ADVENTURES OF THE ARTIFICIAL WOMAN

A NOVEL

THOMAS BERGER

SIMON & SCHUSTER

NEW YORK LONDON TORONTO SYDNEY

SIMON & SCHUSTER
Rockefeller Center
1230 Avenue of the Americas
New York, NY 10020

SIMON & SCHUSTER and colophon are registered trademarks
of Simon & Schuster, Inc.

For information regarding special discounts for bulk purchases,
please contact Simon & Schuster Special Sales at
1-800-456-6798 or business@simonandschuster.com

Manufactured in the United States of America

10 9 8 7 6 5 4 3 2 1

Library of Congress Cataloging-in-Publication Data

Berger, Thomas, 1924–
Adventures of the artificial woman : a novel / Thomas Berger.
p.   cm.
1. Women—United States—Fiction. 2. Man-woman
relationships—Fiction. 3. Artificial intelligence—Fiction.
4. Women in politics—Fiction. 5. Robotics—Fiction.
6. Robots—Fiction. I. Title.
PS3552.E719A65 2004
813'.54—dc22   2003065027
ISBN 0-7432-5740-5

To David W. Madden

1

Never having found a real woman with whom he could sustain a more than temporary connection, Ellery Pierce, a technician at a firm that made animatronic creatures for movie studios and theme parks, decided to fabricate one from scratch.

The artificial woman would naturally be able to perform every function, but sex was the least of what Pierce looked for in his made-to-order model. He had never had undue difficulty in finding live females to satisfy his erotic appetites. He was witty, considerate, and instinctively affectionate. Physically he was trim and fit, curly haired, clear-eyed; in his smile generosity and impudence were combined with a hint of reproach. The reproach was for the many women he had known who, having soon exhausted an early attraction, on longer acquaintance found him wanting.

For years he had made a sincere effort to determine the reason for this state of affairs and, if the fault proved his own, to seek a personal change. But the fact was that no matter how hard he tried, he could not honestly blame himself. Obviously he bore no responsibility for having been reared by a single mother who adored and spoiled her only child, a child who was therefore led to expect much the same treatment from the other examples of the female sex he would encounter after leaving the nest.

In which expectation he was proven wrong rather sooner than later. There were some women who immediately disliked or were indifferent to him, but they were easier to deal with than those who at the outset seemed to regard meeting him as at least a positive experience and sometimes even life-enhancing, to the degree that they might subsequently insist they were in love. In such cases he often responded in kind, and by the time he was thirty-three he had lived, respectively, with three such persons and had been married to two of them. Each of these associations had come to an unhappy end, and though he was first to admit to being imperfect, he believed his only major flaw was an inability to choose the right partner.

It took forever to dawn on him that, anyway in his case, there were no right ones. Eventually the most amiable would turn sarcastic, make aspersions on his tastes, oppose his opinions, disrespect his judgments, and in general be an adversary instead of an ally. No doubt some men did not mind that sort of thing or, more likely, felt they had no alternative to making the best of the situation, but Pierce was not of their company. He suspected the solution might well be not, so to speak, human but rather technological.

The materials by which artificial creatures could be made were available at his place of work, where one of the current projects was the construction of animatronic orangutans for a movie to be set in Borneo. Real animals would be used extensively in the picture, but however well trained, they were not altogether reliable in certain stunts involving actors. With their natural reluctance (though not, in apes, an inability) to distinguish make-believe from reality, live orangutans were, in the violent scenes, capable of mistaking the man who played the villain as the genuine article, maiming him if not worse. Pierce's special-effects company could produce imitation orangs so lifelike as to fool their living counterparts at as close as twenty paces, and who knows how far they might have gone had a female animatron been supplied with a sex organ sprayed with the scent from a real animal in heat?

The firm had less experience with the simulation of human beings. In the movies robots and of course "cyborgs" are depicted by actors made up to resemble automata, not the other way around. In theme-park exhibits the animated mannequins make only limited, prescribed movements, and their voices, if any, are those of amplified electronic sound systems. To fabricate a woman who could be put to all the uses of a real one, and fool everyone but her creator, Pierce had his work cut out for him. But he was a journeyman at the craft, and he was persistent once he had defined a result short of achieving which he could quit without forsaking his life.

The effort would have been demanding enough could he have pursued it openly and full-time—the selection of synthetic skin alone took years—but he had to continue in his regular job as well, if only to ensure access to the materials and equipment with which to fashion the artificial woman. In fact Pierce did better than that, so proficiently that in time he was appointed head of the research department, in which post he enjoyed many privileges and immunities helpful to his private project, coming and going as he wished, in all areas of the plant, at moments of his own choosing. The night watchman would never ask why he was there at three A.M., nor see what he was doing.

Pierce was in his mid-forties when, after many failures, diversions, and interim stages, he had at last produced a creature in whom he had sufficient confidence to introduce her to another human being. He chose the postman who delivered mail to the rural box at his weekend hideaway, to which he had begun to bring the artificial woman in disassembled form six months before. He had put her together there and conducted many private trial runs, some even outside, for he had no near neighbors and the house was at the end of a long lane on which a car could be heard as soon as it turned off the county road.

The mailman, in his right-hand-drive vehicle, would swoop onto the shoulder for only an instant in which to thrust a rolled newspaper into the box before accelerating away. Counting on him to serve as the perfect short-lived audience for the maiden event, Pierce led the woman down the dirt lane at the normal pace of a human being strolling on such a surface. After much work and many adjustments, her stride was at last flawless. While an ability to run at full speed had been relatively easy to develop and maintain, a simple walk was very difficult to accomplish, owing to the problem of equilibrium, a more complex process than one remembers, though every mortal eventually masters it as a child.

While they waited at roadside, Pierce made small talk with his creation, whose responses were activated by the sound of another voice. Phyllis could draw from a bank of several dozen programmed phrases, and she also had the capacity to learn new ones as she heard them. When he now said, "It's warm for March," and she answered, "Spring is early this year," he decided to provide her further with, "I saw some crocuses in the side yard."

The postman was a punctual fellow, his Jeep vaulting over the camelback a hundred yards to the east at 10:02. When he braked at the mailbox, Pierce said, "Good morning, Rollie. I don't think you've met my wife, Phyllis."

"Didn't even know you were married," said the man, teeth gleaming. He nodded. "Ma'am."

"This is Rollie, Phyl," said Pierce.

Phyllis smiled prettily. "I'm pleased to meet you, Rollie," said she. "I've heard so much about you."

The postman's brow showed a furrow. "You *have?*"

Pierce intruded, taking the extended newspaper. "We just got married last week, in town."

"I'll bet you will be real happy," Rollie said, nodding some more with his balding head and fat shoulders. He gunned the engine and sped away.

Phyllis's maiden appearance had been an unqualified success! Pierce was gratified. He yearned briefly for someone with whom to celebrate his triumph, but he had only Phyllis. He could never take a living person into his confidence on this matter, for doing so would nullify his purpose in building the robot—a truth that first occurred to him only at that moment. He was stuck with Phyllis for good or ill, much as a mother is responsible for a child she has borne, with the difference that it would not be criminal for Pierce to neglect, discard, or even destroy the creature he had made, in any of which circumstances he would be guilty only of wasting much of his life.

"Well, Phyl, it's up to us," he said when, back in the house, he opened a bottle of champagne and poured them each a glass.

"Here's to us, Ellery," said she, and, as she had been pro-grammed, lifted the flute to her delicate pink lips and quaffed from it. Her throat was a waterproofed tube that debouched into a collection chamber in the abdominal area. She was capable of eating real food, even masticating dense meats, all of which de-scended to the same chamber, which could be removed for emp-tying through swingaway buttocks, hinged inconspicuously.

"What do you think, Phyl? Are we ready to go to bed?"

She smiled, with a sensual glint in her hazel eyes, and breathily moaned, "God, how I want you, Ellery."

But every time she repeated that statement it sounded less provocative, perhaps because he had continued to drink more champagne and, unlike her, was affected by it.

"Maybe I should have you talk dirty," he told her when the bottle was almost empty and his disappointment had accumu-lated.

"I would like that." This was the stock phrase, applied to anything he said with a certain inflection. It was not appropri-ate here, sounding like mockery.

"Don't respond for a while, Phyllis. I'm trying to think, and I'm somewhat drunk. I haven't had any alcohol for a long time."

Displaying a sympathetic expression that was remarkably believable, she remained silent as ordered.

Pierce was suddenly almost overcome with an emotion that, consciously anyhow, was not simple self-admiration. "I've never known a woman who would not use such an opportunity to get the knife in—I mean, if she herself was sober as you are. If she too was drunk—well, usually they've been loud. I can't stand noisy women, Phyl. They haven't the voices for it. They tend to be screechy. I've given you a soft voice of the kind I like. Say something now."

"I'm really enjoying myself," said she and caressed him lightly on the wrist with velvety fingers, the tips of which were, as in humans, cool, but her palm was warm. After many trials he had arrived at a system that could maintain the right temperature through the circulation of warm oil, heated by a system that had its own dedicated source of power. The storage batteries that provided the other, motile functions would soon have been exhausted by this demand. Periodically warmed by a house-current plug-in, the oil in its insulated conduits would not cool for hours. Whether for all night remained to be determined; thus far Pierce had returned her to the home workshop when he went to bed.

But they had reached a new phase now. It was only around noon, but he was drunk and really for the first time felt sexually attracted to Phyllis in an immediate way, as opposed to the theoretical allure of the planning and construction stages. He had given her breasts of the shape and size he believed perfect, the nose and mouth and silken chestnut hair, the poreless skin, the smooth slender thighs, the curve from waist to hip, the elongated and very narrow shape of foot by which he had always been fascinated. Yet until this moment she had remained a machine, which was to say too flawless to pass as human. A case might well be made that sensuality was a contradiction of the perfect, perfection being complete in itself, needing nobody else.

What was different now was not Phyllis, who could not change, but rather Pierce himself. He swept her up in his arms —at 108, well distributed, she was just the right weight to carry—and bore her into the bedroom, lowered her to the bed, and, leaning, pressed his lips to hers, which triggered her to give him the tongue and put gentle but importunate fingers into his crotch.

He undressed her of the jeans and sweater in which she had met the mailman and tore away the sparkling white underwear with one hand while ripping off his own clothes with the other. Never had he known desire of this intensity, and his ardor was reflected in hers. She clasped and plucked and sighed, tossing her head violently on the pillow, moaning, "God, how I want you, Ellery."

But about to make entry, Pierce all at once deflated. What a foolish phrase! It was something a robot might be programmed to say. That it was said in an acceptable voice, and not a metallic, reverberative tone, suggested an intentional parody.

Driving back to town early Monday morning, a trip that for three-quarters of its duration was in bumper-tight traffic, Pierce had, as always, optimum time for reflection. He had made a mistake in taking Phyllis to bed before she had been properly furnished with the other attributes he sought in the perfect woman, those with which he had erroneously, sentimentally credited her when he was drunk. On the other hand, she should never be treated as a sex object—for the sake of his self-respect, not hers; *she* was a machine.

At the moment, deprived of her integrity, Phyllis rode in a metal box in the rear of his Land Rover, disassembled into several large parts, a measure Pierce felt he should take lest an accident lead to her discovery.

His home in town was in a high-rise building, and transferring Phyllis from the basement garage to a tenth-floor apartment was a demanding exercise, but he had been doing it successfully and unobtrusively for years. Throughout the phases of her construction he had kept her in disparate parts throughout the week, in the locked crate, inside a walk-in bedroom closet, which was also locked against the possible intrusions of maintenance personnel or the weekly cleaning woman.

Now, as he wheeled the crate over the threshold, he made a bold decision. He liberated the head, thorax, and limbs from their imprisonment and assembled Phyllis right there on the living room rug. For the first time her nudity was embarrassing to him, though not of course to her.

"Have to put some clothes on you," he said. For some months he had been purchasing by noncompromising internet or mail a wardrobe appropriate to a woman of her apparent age, which he placed at, give or take, twenty-five. "Go on to the bedroom." She had taken only a step or two before he corrected himself. "Sorry, Phyl. You've never seen it, have you? It's at the end of that hallway. Why don't you go on ahead while I put this stuff away."

She had stopped and turned gracefully at the first word. "That would be nice."

He watched the movement of her exquisite behind as she left the room, but as sculptor, not lecher. He could not have done better there, though perhaps improvement might still be made in that transitional area between the back-of-the-knee and the developing swell of the calf. Her stride was a fluid marvel, justifying the grief it had caused him.

He left the carrying case and hand truck where they were and followed her to the bedroom. Having had no further instructions, Phyllis stood facing him in the middle of the room, at the foot of the bed. She was lovely, if he did say so himself, but not gorgeous in the way that would on first sight enflame men and infuriate other women. She was more sleek than voluptuous. Even so, were her breasts a bit too full?

He weighed them in his hands. They were at room temperature, the heating element not having been charged since the
day before, and he felt no desire while manipulating them.

"I think they're just right, Phyl, at least for now."

"That's nice."

"Elaine told me she once had an orgasm when the doctor did
this at her annual exam."

"Elaine was your first wife."

"The doctor was a woman."

"I see," said Phyllis.

Pierce let go of her breasts. "Elaine wasn't a Lesbian. She
said that only to insult me."

"She," Phyllis said smugly, "was not nice."

"You," Pierce felt enormous satisfaction in telling her, "will
never need to be examined by any kind of doctor. You can't
get sick, and you can't die. You will never have a menstrual
period. . . . Don't say either 'That's nice' or 'I see.' Get something else from the bank."

She nodded smartly. "Bite me."

He whooped with laughter. "I forgot all about that one! I put
it there as a joke. You're not supposed to say it to me, though."

"I'm sorry."

"Don't be," he said unthinkingly, as if he were being considerate with a human being. "You haven't done anything wrong.
Now I'm going to dress you and then go to work. No more lock-
ing you up in parts all week. That had begun to depress me,
even if it had no effect on you."

Probably because of his negative reaction to her previous
utterance, Phyllis remained silent, standing there naked at the
foot of the bed, looking too much like a window dummy.

"Okay, Phyl, do something. It's too weird when you're like that."

"What do you want me to do, Ellery?"

"Try to dress yourself," said he. "Get your underwear from the top drawer of the bureau."

He was pleased to see she could put one leg into the briefs while balancing on the other. Not only were her limbs satin-smooth and would never need depilation or know scars, but they would stay in that condition. If the skin was damaged in any way, it could be repaired with an invisible patch.

"Let's try something, Phyl. There are a couple of boxes on the floor of the closet. Go through them yourself and pick out something to wear at home all day. I'm going to leave you here when I go to work."

In a few efficient moments she was wearing shorts striped in blue and a pink shirt and was shod in backless tan sandals, an appropriate outfit for the occasion and temperature, and though probably not what Pierce himself would have selected at this moment, altogether suitable. He was impressed by her ability to make a reasonable choice of this simple kind.

"You look very nice."

An immediate difference between Phyllis and a real woman was her utter lack of interest in his approval of her attire. She nodded politely and said, "Yes." With both his wives and all his girlfriends Pierce could by praising their taste in clothing some-times win back at least some of the points he lost elsewhere. This was quite another thing than "How beautiful you are when you're mad," which tended to infuriate, whereas he was con-vinced there were times when a man might find an advantage in saying, "You're a selfish bitch but I have to admit you have an eye for fabrics." That this might sound gay could only help further.

His plans for Phyllis were founded on the wisdom of half a lifetime. "You should show modest pleasure when you are complimented. A thank-you and a smile will do it. . . . See that leather box over there? Get the string of cultured pearls from inside and put them around your neck. I like an elegant touch with a simple outfit. Earrings wouldn't look right."

This was one of those times when speaking to her seemed no more than talking to himself, though her eyes were brightly fastened to his, her lips parted ever so slightly, her head tilted in the attitude of the intent listener. Nevertheless he went on. "Your skin is flawless. That might not be completely realistic but it's a personal taste of mine since I was a teenager and saw how the prettiest girls could be ruined by facial eruptions."

Phyllis stared toward the window on the far side of the bed. "Look at the sunshine. What a nice day."

He had lost her now, which was probably just as well. He did not need a collaborator on so personal a project, not even if it were his own creation. A Ferrari does not help tune its own engine.

When Pierce returned from work in the early evening, Phyllis was still seated in the basket-chair in which he had left her that morning. He would not kiss her hello, her lips having been without warmth all day. It would be unsafe to leave the heating system plugged in unless he were at hand. Though she might be instructed to pull the plug at the first sign of disfunction, placing complete trust in any machine would be at least as unwise as trusting any of his living women had proven. True responsibility was a rare virtue in life or laboratory. So, anyway, he believed it prudent to assume.

Phyllis was where he had left her, but she now wore the burgundy-colored silk dress he had added to her wardrobe after scanning upscale catalogues for images that appealed to him. She had become more beautiful than he designed her to be, indeed than he thought he wanted her to be until he saw her now. She had done something to her hair that was difficult to define, pulling some of it back and piling some high, and had subtly altered her natural coloring, presumably through makeup though he had provided none.

She sprang up, kissing him with warm, moist lips that were another happy surprise. She helped him remove his jacket, and she hung it in the doorside closet.

"You plugged in the heater yourself?" He asked about the least of her accomplishments because it was the easiest to understand. She had, after all, seen him do it.

Phyllis whirled away to the little bar in the corner near the passageway to the kitchen. "Tell me if I've got the lime juice right." She added ice from the bucket to a little china pitcher and swirled it vigorously.

"You're making gimlets?"

She brought one to him, holding her own aside until he tasted his.

"It's perfect," said he. "Not too cold, and just right with the *gin*, not vodka. I hate vodka." He savored a second sip, playing for time in which to decide how best to question her artificial intelligence without discouraging her, or it.

"So, Phyl, what kind of day did you have?" He sat down on the sofa and patted the cushion next to him. But she failed to get the message, or defied it, choosing a chair instead, in fact one on the other side of the plate-glass coffee table onto which she lowered her as yet untasted drink.

"I cleaned the apartment," said she. "When I saw I had done a good job, I called the woman whom you hire and discharged her."

"You *what?*"

"Yes, Ellery," said Phyllis, nodding. "She would be redundant."

Pierce felt a fearful premonition, brief as a momentary draft from a remote window, but moved aggressively to override it. "You take a lot on yourself, Phyllis."

"I'll call her back."

"No." He took the last swallow in the shallow glass. "That's okay. Let's see how it works out. Meanwhile I'll pay Celine anyway. She's a single mother and needs the money."

"She told me she was thinking of dropping *you*," Phyllis said. "Her schedule's too full."

"That's probably pride."

"I can't identify pride. Maybe I'm spelling it incorrectly."

"No," said Pierce, pleased to find just the right excuse to make a telling point. "You will never understand that concept. You are a machine, Phyllis. You can't have pride any more than you can feel pain."

"But I know what pain is, Ellery, even if I can't feel it. I am aware that *you* can feel it and that I am not to cause you any, even though I am stronger than you."

"You're dreaming." It occurred to Pierce to swap his empty glass for her full one, which it really made no sense for her to drink anyway. He was already getting the effect of the first gimlet. "You're *not* stronger than me. I can literally take you apart any time I want."

She appeared to be deliberating. "You're right, Ellery," she said finally, winking at him. "I wasn't serious. I was lying."

"No, you weren't, Phyl. Machines have no sense of irony and therefore never joke and never lie. You were simply trying to take power. Automobiles try that from time to time, with sticking accelerators, brakes that fail, and so on. . . . If you don't want your drink, I'll take it."

"Of course, Ellery." She brought it around the coffee table to him.

"Sit down here, Phyllis." When she did so, primly keeping her knees together, Pierce praised the first gimlet and drank half the second, then distended his nostrils. "I smell food. Did you phone for that, too?"

"Yes." Her eyes looked as real as any could, though he had installed them with his own two hands helped by needlenosed pliers and tweezers, and they were attached within not to a brain but rather a compact computer, access to which was offered by a little trapdoor in her crown. "I dialed the numbers in your book: the liquor store, market, the drugstore."

Pierce had quickly finished the second drink. He stood up with authority. "I'd better eat before I get too drunk on my empty stomach. I passed up lunch. We were testing a new servo motor, smaller even than the ones in you, Phyl. About the size of a thumb, but not very durable."

"I want to hear all about your work, Ellery."

They went hand in hand to the dining area, where, before she detached herself to enter the kitchen, Pierce asked, "How did you pay for the stuff you had delivered?"

"I signed for it. I took the credit-card numbers off the receipts in your desk."

"What name did you use?"

"Phyllis Pierce."

He frowned and asked, as much of himself as of her, "Are you my wife?"

"That was how you introduced me to the mailman. Was I wrong?"

"No, that's fine." He was proud of the supple figure he had given her, as she stood in the doorway to the kitchen, looking gracefully back over a silk shoulder.

Seated at dinner, he asked, "Where in the world did you find a restaurant that makes pot roast?"

"*Boeuf braisé*," said Phyllis. "I followed the cookbook."

"What cookbook?"

"*French Cuisine for Dummies*, which I ordered from a bookstore that delivers."

"This is first-rate, Phyl," Pierce said, savoring the dark thick gravy's marriage with the buttery mashed potatoes.

"You can't lose with the best ingredients and care in their preparation." Phyllis had filled a plate for herself but had not tasted of it.

"Are you quoting from somebody?"

"I heard that on the Food Channel." She fingered the rim of her plate. "Would you like me to eat this?"

"I can't see the point in it. But you were right to fill the plate. It looks better that way."

"I could empty myself, Ellery. You wouldn't have to see it."

"Thanks all the same, Phyl. That system's for use only when we eat with other people." After the preprandial drinks and several glasses of a hearty pinot noir, Pierce no longer thought it odd to thank a robot for an offered courtesy and to make an apologetic explanation. Thus far, in all the ways that counted, Phyllis was an admirable surrogate for a woman. Indeed she did a better job at it than any real one with whom he had associated, except of course his mother, one of whose many culinary specialties had been pot roast—and Phyllis's mashed potatoes were better. Her roasted baby carrots with thyme and frenched green beans with almonds were unique in his experience.

"I like to be with you, Ellery."

"I enjoy just the two of us, too—uh, also." He did not want to confuse her in matters of language. "But I look forward to our having a social life. My wives sooner or later ruined that. One always drank too much and picked a quarrel, if not with me, then with other women. And I once caught a girlfriend of mine making out with some other guy in a pantry off a kitchen."

"Making out?"

"Kissing, fondling, necking."

"It shouldn't be done?" ·

"You should just dance with the guy that brung you."

"I don't understand that idiom."

"My fault, Phyl. It's folksy jargon, referring to fidelity." She was capable of adding to her memory bank anything she heard, but he suggested she disregard this one and resumed. "I'm going to invite some people to a dinner party here, Friday or Saturday night. We'll stay in town next weekend, barring any malfunctions. You're performing so well. Thus far I don't see any need for finer tuning. I want to go for broke. I've waited so long."

"I'm at your service, Ellery." Phyllis showed the smile that made so much of a pouty lower lip, which, not a professional sculptor, he had labored so hard to fashion.

2

Pierce had no real friends, having been too obsessed with his private project to make any, and he did not wish, at least at this time, to expose Phyllis to any of his colleagues from work. They might recognize some of her attributes as being other than human. If one of her systems faltered, the lay witness might not even notice, were corrective measures taken quickly. But an experienced animatronic technician would be hard to fool in the presence of certain effects, subtle alterations in the rhythm of movement, the slightest of hesitations, the least variation in balance, or of course any change in her sound system: Robotic personages do not become hoarse by any natural means.

A guest list was therefore not easy to compile. Eventually he came up with four persons: Janet and Tyler Hallstrom, the nearest neighbors along the hall, whom Pierce had known not well but routinely during the recent years of his residency, and his gay acquaintance Cliff, met first at the gym and never since known better than as a fellow at the juice bar, with whom in shared generalities he had always been at pains to keep free of personal implication, as had Cliff, who furthermore was extremely modest when showering. Pierce knew he was homosexual only because Cliff said so once, with the same self-possession with which he might have said he was Italian. When he invited Cliff to dinner, Pierce made it for two, learning for the first time that Cliff had a regular partner named Ray.

These men arrived at the same moment as the Hallstroms, which caused a traffic jam at the threshold but made it convenient to introduce Phyllis to all the guests at once.

Janet Hallstrom proved to be a demonstrative woman, who hugged and kissed the new "wife," crying, "When did *this* happen?"

And even before seizing his hand, Cliff chided Pierce for keeping the new marriage a surprise till now and presented him with a bottle of chenin blanc that would have been champagne if he had only known. Ray's handshake was even more crushing than Cliff's. He exchanged smiles with Phyllis, who had not yet learned to offer a physical greeting. Fortunately she had not been flustered by Janet's.

Tyler Hallstrom, fair, tall, bony, prematurely balding, leered at Phyllis, though whether lasciviously or simply in the spirit of the moment remained to be proved. She certainly looked good in the white pants and paisley blouse Pierce had chosen for her. He realized that he would have to alter her hair slightly from time to time if they saw the same people often, though there were women—Janet Hallstrom among them—who always maintained the same do. A bit hefty, with blunt features and a narrow mouth, Janet was not unattractive but would never turn a head.

When they withdrew to the dining area after preliminary

drinks at the other end of the room, with visits to the terrace to toast the lights of the city on such a clement evening, Pierce seated Hallstrom between himself at the head of the table and Ray, the purpose being to keep the heterosexual neighbor from putting too much scrutiny on Phyllis, something Ray was unlikely to do. On the other side, it was Cliff who flanked her, Janet at Pierce's right elbow.

Phyllis, unassisted, brought the hot dishes from the kitchen. Pierce wanted to keep her moving, though the inevitable moment came when everything was in place and she had to sit down and face the music—as if it were she who had to handle the strain! He was so nervous he all but cut himself while carving the crown roast of lamb, though the dish, not she, was the cynosure.

"What's the stuffing?" asked Ray, who turned out to be the cook of the pair, though he was the brawnier, with the jaw of a lineman.

"A forcemeat of minced lamb," Phyllis said.

"And this is—fennel?" asked Janet, passing the dish. "What a beautiful menu, Phyllis."

A mashed-potato lookalike turned out to be a puree of parsnips, scented and delicate. Pierce was at one with the others in never having heard of it. Phyllis was grandstanding as a new-lywed. Was that good or bad? At the moment everybody was distracted by the food, but Janet's nose was probably en route to being out of joint. Pierce had heard Hallstrom praise her cook-ery, of which, skinny as he was, he hardly served as advertise-ment.

It took no more than one taste for Cliff to raise his glass to Phyllis, a gesture soon duplicated by the others. "This," said he, "would be well worth a detour, as the French say."

To which Hallstrom responded, "Hear, hear."

"Please admit it, Phyllis," said Janet. "You're on a professional level."

Phyllis replied with her quote about the best ingredients, which seemed to go over well with the men, but Janet balked, fending off the comment with raised fingers that, Pierce noted, were exquisitely shaped. Perhaps he could have done a better job with Phyllis's, not that anything was wrong with those she was now using to "eat" the meal she had prepared so well.

"Please," Janet was saying. "I can overcook the finest organic veggies from the best boutique farms. You ask Tyler."

Fearing that Phyllis might not be able to elude Janet's bitchy trap, which was really designed for its effect on Hallstrom—who between forkfuls was seemingly trying to catch the eye of the artificial woman—Pierce stepped in.

"Tyler brags about your prowess in the kitchen. Let's say both he and I have wonderful wives."

"As do I," Cliff noted without bravado or defiance.

Ray thanked him and then confessed to Phyllis that about all he could do that could be counted on was broiled steak.

Now Pierce's fear was that his animatronic spouse would innocently say something that could be taken the wrong way by the sensitive, but before he could intrude again, Phyllis said, "Then I want some pointers from you. I've never cooked steak."

Janet frowned suspiciously, the corrugated forehead doing nothing for her looks.

"We eat steak only in the country," Pierce explained, "where I man the barbecue."

"I want the recipes for everything," Ray announced. "It's high time I get more ambitious. I want to say right now, the next get-together must be at *our* house."

Everyone but Pierce assented with enthusiasm, including Phyllis. Pierce wondered whether he had made a mistake in having come up with the idea to expose her to society in this fashion. He did not want them—her and him—to acquire regular friends, if not ever, at least not yet. It was true that thus far she had performed spectacularly well, but even human beings have their lapses. If Phyllis had one, the game might be up in an instant.

Her batteries obviously were holding their charge, else she would have retired temporarily to the back bathroom and replaced them with fresh units, as she was programmed to do when it was necessary, a little backup dry-cell system providing enough power to effect the switch. Nevertheless, Pierce felt it prudent to make the exchange before one became crucial, and he suggested as much when the guests had adjourned to the upholstered furniture for coffee and Phyllis and he were alone for a moment in the kitchen.

"All right, Ellery," she said, turned quickly, and collapsed to the floor.

The fall made little noise but was sufficiently violent to have had serious implications. Helping her to her feet, Pierce made a quick inspection by eye and touch and found nothing amiss, but whether internal damage had been done would be difficult to ascertain without a more thorough examination than was practicable at the moment. Yet allowing her to resume her full role as hostess would be risky.

It was of course nonsensical to ask how she felt, but he did so anyway.

"I'm fine."

Though he had only himself to blame, Pierce spoke irritably.

"You don't know how you are, Phyl. Are you even aware you just fell down?"

"That's too bad."

"Lift both arms, twisting the wrists, then lower them. . . . Spin in place. . . . Your equilibrium doesn't seem to be affected. What's the sum of six and eight?"

"Fourteen," she answered promptly, but quickly corrected herself. "Or fifteen. Whatever."

He repeated the question and heard still another answer. "Maybe twenty-seven. Who gives a shit?"

Another phrase he had, unwisely, given her as a joke, at a time when he could not have envisioned a future juncture of this sort. But he refused to panic. "Go to the bedroom and close the door."

"All right, Ellery."

He observed Phyllis's stride as she walked down the hall and saw nothing irregular. It seemed he was in luck: her "mental" problems, involving only a chip or two, were much more easily dealt with than the subtle physical functions.

He returned to his guests and made the announcement. "I'm sorry. Phyllis isn't feeling well all of a sudden. She's had to go lie down."

"Can I help?" offered Janet, producing a sympathetic knit of eyebrow, an effect Phyllis could not as yet display. Pierce was learning a lot by watching a real woman at close range. Of course there were female colleagues and employees to observe at work, but the conditions were distracting.

"A little rest will do the trick, I'm sure," said he. "She exhausted herself on this meal."

"Poor baby," groaned Ray. "I can imagine."

Cliff modestly echoed his partner's sentiments, but Hallstrom showed the most dismay of all, his long jaw falling.

"Go to her, Janet," said he, and before Pierce, now pouring wine at the other side of the table, could block the route, Janet did as asked. She was more than halfway along the short hall when Pierce reached its entrance. He could only bring up the rear as she found the right door on her first try, opening it and plunging within, whining, "Darling Phyllis, it's Janet. How—"

Pierce arrived just as his animatronic wife delivered a powerful punch to Janet's jaw, knocking their neighbor to the floor. He knelt to determine whether the woman was still alive, as she proved to be though altogether unconscious.

He rose. "You're out of control, Phyl. I'm going to have to dismantle you."

"All right, Ellery," she said with normal submissiveness, but when he came near enough she threw at him the same sort of punch that had felled Janet, but missed by a considerable distance though at a similar range. This failure of spatial perception indicated that her further deterioration was occurring as he watched.

"Would you like to have sex?"

"Sit down in that chair over there, Phyllis. I'm going to pull your brain."

"I'll kick your ass, Ellery."

"What you're doing now comes from the movies you undoubtedly watched in between the cooking shows. The characters are poor models for you, Phyl. They're not real. Now sit down. You know this doesn't hurt." It might be foolish to speak so to a machine, but the reassurance was mostly for himself.

He was seized from behind by someone with steel forearms and lifted off his feet, his toes impotently kicking air.

"Kill Janet, Phyllis," said his captor. "I'll throw Ellery off the terrace."

"Hallstrom?" Pierce asked, in a kind of scream. "What's wrong with you? Let me go!"

"Get her, Phyl!" shouted Hallstrom. "She's coming to."

Pierce was struggling, but though no weakling, in Hallstrom's grasp he was like a small, wriggling dog.

"No," Phyllis said. "Let Ellery go." She wore an expression that Pierce had never seen before. It must have been something else she had learned that afternoon, perhaps from a soap opera: strong, resolute, yet understanding.

On the floor Janet lived up to Hallstrom's prediction and became fully conscious and, shortly thereafter, vocal. "Stop that immediately, Tyler!" she ordered even as she was struggling to her feet. Hallstrom immediately withdrew his clamping arms from Pierce's waist.

Rubbing the jaw where she had taken the blow, Janet took charge of the situation. "Tyler, you go sit down on the bed." Hallstrom proceeded hastily to do so, looking quite as gangly, balding, and harmless as he had at table. She turned to Pierce.

"Are you okay, Ellery?"

He was badly shaken up, though not physically damaged. "I am not sure." He glared at Hallstrom, who seemed to be smiling. "He talked about *killing* me—and also you! For God's sake, Janet."

"I know, it's over the line," she said. "Crises happen. You'll find out, but right now you're new to the situation."

At that moment Cliff and Ray dashed in together, Cliff asking, "*What's* going on here, people?"

To which Ray added, "Is anyone hurt? Tyler?"

"I'm fine," said he. "Never been better."

"Phyllis?"

She displayed a sweet smile. "Kiss my ass."

Unfazed, Ray told Cliff, "It's nice that nobody got hurt."

Pierce addressed his guests. "I apologize. She's having some problems. If you'll all adjourn to the living room, I'll be there in a minute."

"Probably just a faulty relay," Janet told him. "I've gone through that many times with Tyler. At first I used to panic, until I found that even in a malfunction I always have the upper hand. He talks of killing me, but it's necessarily just talk. He's incapable of doing anything I haven't ordered him to do."

Cliff wore a radiant grin for Pierce's benefit. "You're new at the game, Ellery. Ray and I have been together for four years now, and he still can be a troublemaker, but Janet's right: What can he do except what I tell him?"

Pierce stared at Phyllis, who stood at an angle from him that was exaggerated in the mirror above the dresser, so that in the glass she was apparently looking in the wrong direction, but he addressed Cliff and Janet. "You're saying that Ray and Hallstrom are animatronic figures too?"

While Cliff nodded sympathetically, Janet answered. "I could tell you didn't know."

"Whereas both of you knew immediately with Phyllis."

"You'll be like that too after a while," said Cliff.

"Oh, sure, Ellery," Janet said. "It's like riding a bike. You are able to do it all of a sudden."

"I *made* her," Pierce cried. "I built her from scratch. That's my profession, but it took years. Where'd you get yours?" His swiveling stare embraced them both.

Janet responded first. "I bought Tyler on eBay some time ago."

Cliff produced a bubbling chuckle. "Ray belonged to my former partner. We shared him for a while before Terry decided I preferred Ray to him and walked out." He smirked. "He was absolutely right! Ray doesn't need constant reassurance. Ray doesn't have feelings that can be hurt. Ray doesn't have to work out to keep in shape."

Ray showed no reaction to these comments.

"My first husband," said Janet, "was a loser at everything he tried, but he insisted on *participating* all the same, entering the competition. The result was he lost everything he had and everything I had. If he could only have accepted his lot in life! But then he would have been Tyler."

"Just a moment," said Pierce. "It was that nonhuman paragon of yours who wanted to murder me."

She shrugged. "How often has your computer crashed, your car refused to start, the washer/dryer gone out of order? Now and again a giant construction crane topples over, a nuclear submarine self-destructs."

"Those are accidents, usually because of human error, never involving intention, volition, or malice."

Janet shook her head. "How can we say that? Who knows what goes on in the circuits of a machine? I've been observing Tyler at close hand for three years now, and I'll admit I probably don't really know him yet. Maybe I never will." She tossed her hair. "Let's see what kind of father he is."

"Oh," Cliff cried, "you're pregnant? Congratulations!"

Janet simpered. "We're trying, with a sperm donor. But Tyler does the rest." She blushed. "I never knew what lovemaking was until I got Tyler. Of course he never loses energy."

Cliff cleared his throat in a conspicuously discreet fashion. "Modesty forbids my boasting about Ray, but—" He gleefully threw up his hands.

"Well, all right," Pierce said to Janet. "You can control Tyler when you're with him. But surely you can't send him out by himself?"

"We go to work together, at our own business: Hallstrom Investment Counseling."

"Ray's home all day. He's no problem," said Cliff. "I check in by phone or e-mail from time to time, but that's only because I get lonely for someone who amuses me. The people I work with are hopeless."

"All right, all right," said Pierce, who had lost his patience. "I've had enough of this. I'm going to ask you all to leave."

"Please don't be angry with me, Ellery," said Janet, her lips sagging woefully. "Nothing actually happened."

Cliff complained, "Ray and I are hardly at fault."

Pierce felt ruthless. "Just get out, all of you, and take your damn robots with you."

Cliff and Ray hastily departed. Janet, however, lingered and, coming closer to Pierce, said gently, "We oughtn't be at odds, living so close. Maybe we should get to know each other, just you and I, two people." Her gesture took in both Phyllis, standing silently in the same position as earlier, and Hallstrom, who sat on the edge of the bed, apparently studying the floor. "The convenient thing about *them* is they couldn't care less."

Pierce had no personal interest in her. He was obsessed with the recent threat on his life. "*Why*," he asked, "did he want to kill me?"

"I'm not saying they don't have *any* emotions." Janet took his hand. "But what good would they be if they were totally blank?"

Keeping an eye on Hallstrom as he did so, Pierce freed himself. "There's something wrong with you. Please leave."

She gave him what was probably intended to be a beseeching look, but did as told, Hallstrom striding blithely ahead of her.

When they were alone, Pierce again asked Phyllis how she was feeling.

"I'm okay now, Ellery."

"You did a fine job tonight. It wasn't your fault that it ended as it did. Please don't take offense if I have to overhaul you."

"I couldn't. I'm not a person."

"Anybody could stumble and take a spill. I've done it myself."

"Yes."

"The fall probably jarred your systems, hence the strange things you did and said."

She smiled with her lustrous eyes and lush mouth. "I did that on purpose. I wanted them to leave so we could have sex."

Pierce frowned. "You tried to punch me."

"I was just putting a little spice into our relationship."

He winced at the mirror. The matter of his identity was troubling. Insofar as she had any existence beyond the plastics and metals that made up her body, Phyllis was, necessarily, himself. If her soul was other than a version of his, then *she* was the person and he the animatron. Yet if he was capable of such reflection, an exercise peculiar to human beings, he was not a machine.

"You're full of surprises," he told her. "You've proven to be much more complex than I expected. I created you, yet I don't know what you'll do next."

"I'll keep you guessing, Ellery."

She led him to the bed and, after disrobing him, used the belt, tie, and socks to fasten his wrists and ankles to the bedstead.

He had tolerated this through a natural curiosity as to how far she would go, and realized he was fixed helplessly supine only after it was too late to do anything about it but complain.

"I don't find this sexually stimulating, Phyllis. That you came up with the idea is impressive—if that's the right word— but I'm uncomfortable. I want to be untied."

Phyllis had remained fully clothed. She knee-walked to the end of the bed and stepped off. "Sorry, Ellery. I've got you where I want you now. I'm off to a life of new challenges."

He grimaced. "That's more of the foolish crap you picked up from the mass media. You can't make it on your own. You're not some Frankenstein creation of organic materials, with a brain that revolts against its maker. You're an electronic and mechanical personage. You'll need recharging any minute now. And what if one of your systems goes out of order—in fact I think one or more have already done so, or you wouldn't be acting like this."

She extended a lower lip in a never-before-seen pout. "That's your problem, Ellery."

Struggling in vain against his bonds, which unfortunately had been fashioned by Phyllis, who did everything to perfection, Pierce cried, "Where will you go? What will you do?"

She paused with a three-quarter turn in the doorway. "I thought I'd have a try at show business."

"Give me a break!"

She took him literally. "I'll stop off downstairs and tell the super to come up with his passkey and free you."

"Wait a minute, Phyl! I know a lot of movie people. I could put in a word for you."

She spoke seemingly in regret more than reproach. "No, Ellery. I simply couldn't trust you. You constructed me. You'd know countless ways to put me out of commission."

"Tell me, Phyllis. Where did I go wrong? Because I'm going to build another woman, I assure you."

"You left me alone all day. I had to fend for myself."

Pierce could not help admiring what he had made, and he had a change of heart. She had a lot of spunk. "You might find reality different from TV and the internet," he told her paternally. "But remember, you'll always be welcome to come back here, and you can call me at any time you need help. Meanwhile, get the wallet from my jacket pocket. Take the cash and one of the credit cards."

But Phyllis rejected all assistance. "I have to do it on my own, Ellery. That's the point." Without an expression of goodbye, which would reflect a sentiment of which she was incapable, she took leave of her creator.

A feeling of pride overcame any resentment Pierce might have known. He could not reasonably predict how she would fare in the world. She had great strengths: an ability to learn almost instantaneously, from vicarious as well as personal experience; an immunity to irreparable diseases of body and spirit; a lack of spite and other corrosive emotions. Whether they would compensate for the obvious incapacities of a creature who was not what she seemed remained to be proven.

Meanwhile he would begin the construction of Phyllis II. He expected the work to go more quickly this time, now that he was a veteran in the basic phases of the process. The trick would be in the fine-tuning.

3

Pierce began an affair with his neighbor Janet Hallstrom on the day after Phyllis's declaration of independence, which could be seen as his triumph, not only technological but also moral, for he had not opposed her departure. He had created her, but he did not pretend to own her. He qualified as one of the better conceptions of God, in believing which of himself he was being mostly ironic and not threatening the tenets, or lack thereof, of his basic agnosticism.

Janet had applied to Pierce for emotional refuge. After several years of perfection—her characterization of their marriage had not been knowingly false—her animatronic husband had turned brutal.

"You really owe me one," she had come to Pierce's door to insist. "What changed Tyler was meeting that bitch of yours. He hasn't been able to get over the idea that a woman can be man-made, that there are females of his kind."

"Only one so far," Pierce pointed out. He peeped apprehensively down the hall to the Hallstrom door, which remained closed. "I doubt I could subdue him. Can you get me a schematic of his systems? We might have to call the police. Has he hurt you?"

"Only in the feelings," said Janet, "which may seem ridiculous, but when you've gone so long relying on him to act like a human in the good ways but not the bad, and then he shows he's no better than a person of flesh and blood, it destroys something inside." She touched her ample bosom with a thumb.

"Only if you let it be so," said Pierce, emitting one of those platitudes made for such use. It was to avoid involvement with human females that he had created Phyllis, whom suddenly he missed awfully as he had not done until now. It was easy to plan for a Phyllis II, but producing the first model had taken years. Even employing techniques that had been refined through experience and materials greatly improved since the time when he started out, he could not quickly build a new companion.

Janet had fixed him with a penetrating stare from under her thick eyebrows. She was, say, fifteen pounds overweight, and her features were not as precisely shaped as Pierce would have made them had she been a creature of his construction. Her eyes were a bit deliquescent, though that might have been due to her emotional state. One feature that Phyllis and any successor made by Pierce would never have was tear ducts. He believed it likely that women could have legitimate reasons for weeping, but that they actually wept only for effect, having seen it happen too often with his wives. Furthermore, though they might say they liked males who could cry, they were lying. Just try it, and you would hear, "Be a man!"

"Let me fix you a drink," he told Janet.

"I'll get the ice." She beat him to the kitchenette, where she promptly found two glasses and a tray, though more appropriate equipment sat on the little bar she had passed en route and now repaired to.

"No," Pierce said, waving. "No Scotch for me. I'll have a gimlet."

"Oops, too late." She smiled and asked hypocritically, "Do I have to pour it back?"

"Or have it as a refill." He asserted himself with a move to the bar and won this encounter as she, carrying her glass, drifted into the living room and hesitated at the couch.

Phyllis had, first time off the mark, mixed a better gimlet than any he had ever tasted. He nevertheless drank this one, and another, and began a third, Janet meanwhile drowning her troubles in multiple Scotches. They both were soon drunk, a condition that Janet, repellently, called "shitfaced." He found little in her that attracted him, while realizing—despite or perhaps because of the alcohol—that much of what he was not attracted to were human attributes for which Janet could hardly be blamed. You would not catch an animatron wondering what *she* had done that was in any way responsible for an emotional estrangement.

"Should I have been more understanding? They do have feelings, I don't know why, but different from ours, I don't know how." Janet swallowed some Scotch, going at the tumbler as if she would chew its rim. She sat on the couch, while Pierce was in a chair, though not the closest. After another careful gulp she went on. "What I want to ask you, now I've drunk enough— well, I can't find the person who owned Tyler previously and sold him to me: no response to my e-mails." She took another swallow and said quickly, "You are an expert. You built Phyllis."

"Janet, let me speak frankly." Pierce stared rhetorically at the ceiling. "I know nothing about constructing a male. Oh, there may well be certain similarities, eyes, balance, most internal organs, et cetera, but the basic differences are too major to be reconciled. I'll even go so far as to speculate whether there might be greater differences between the sexes with artificial personages than with real." He realized, not with displeasure, that he had never before spoken with anybody human on this subject, unless the exchange of remarks at the showdown the night before could be counted.

"Well," said Janet, not really listening to him, "I've learned my lesson. I—"

"The respective genitals are the least of it, in my opinion. An erectile penis would be relatively easy to make and operate, but the triggering process might be a problem. Throwing a switch would hardly suit a woman." He waited for her response, then asked, "How is arousal simulated in Hallstrom?"

Janet fluttered her hands. "Please. I don't want to hear that name at the moment."

Pierce was annoyed. Why then was she here? "But, as I say, the organs are in themselves not the issue." He took a tongueful of his fourth drink, which now could have been water so far as taste went, his own having been stunned by alcohol, an effect unknown to artificial creatures. "I mean, you can't start with a sexless dummy and then at a certain point install breasts and a vulva and call it female. It has to be a woman from the earliest conception, from the first sketches in what you could call the womb of a computer. That's why Phyllis was such a success, exceeding my conception."

Janet glared at him. "Oh, listen, Ellery, you can talk all you want about how remarkable a machine can be, but they can let you down quite as much as humans can, and then what are you left with? You've given your heart to a hunk of plastic that doesn't have one." Apparently she had been looking angry so as to keep from weeping, and it had not worked.

Pierce hated to see tears. "I'll get you some Kleenex." He rose and hastened to the bedroom, which still smelled of Phyllis—that is, of the perfume he had supplied her, which her own nostrils lacked the capacity to detect, along with any other odor. He had simply forgotten to provide her with a sense of smell. By the hour he was accumulating mental notes for the construction of Phyllis II, but the zest that had inspired and sustained him throughout the making of the first model was hard to reawaken. He had lost the spirit of romance. For example, what occurred to him now was that with sensitized nostrils she could add smoke-detection to her attributes.

"What I need," Janet said, having stolen in silently to encircle his waist from behind and press against him with her abundance of body, "is love."

The experience was in quite another category than the intimate moments he had had with Phyllis, but it was less repugnant than he had supposed, perhaps even more pleasant than not, for unlike the real women he had known in the past, Janet had been voluntarily generous about his performance. She was actually quite a nice person; a few years too old, perhaps, with a slightly crooked lower front tooth and somewhat leathery skin at the clavicles, and even with a reduction in weight her thighs would be sturdier than the ideal, but then he had played no part in her modeling, and her bright eyes would pass, as would her complexion, the subtleties of which would have been difficult to achieve with synthetic tints. Skin coloring had been a problem with Phyllis, if not as major as, say, an orderly yet feminine stride, then more difficult to resolve, for any conclusion must be subjective. Until she walked properly she would fall down, whereas there was no test by which one hue of Caucasian cheek was more natural than the next.

Furthermore after three months Janet had not displayed any of the negative qualities that Pierce had identified in the other real women with whom he had associated. She was not moody, and above all she was not critical of him. He did not mind her self-possession as a successful businessperson. He was not offended by a slight pushiness, demonstrated in her replacing the pillows on his couch with larger and more vivid ones, and it was she who habitually made the choice of restaurants; he cared little about such matters. She never disparaged anything he said, and she had a deft way of stating an opinion or taste that differed greatly from his but did not seem to if considered superficially. He had never yet seen her in that resentful state he thought of as standard for females, perhaps because he contributed in no way to her upkeep, nor did they live together. Maybe that was the trick: their encounters could still be called dates.

Janet continued to share her apartment and in fact her bed with Tyler Hallstrom, though she assured Pierce she was no longer sexually intimate with her animatronic companion. But she did *own* him or it, not to mention that Tyler was her business partner and had a real knack for investment counseling. She feared losing clients if she disposed of him.

"You've helped me think better of myself," she told Pierce. "I'm grateful to you."

He had never heard a woman say that before, and it was very gratifying to him. He determined to program such a sentiment into Phyllis II, which project continued to remain in the note-taking stage despite the need for haste if he was ever to have another artificial woman while he was young enough to make the most of her, but thus far he had been unable to rise above a disabling inhibition. Only several weeks after her departure did he realize he had been in love with Phyllis I.

That feeling grew more profound in the months since he found himself in a condition for which he could use no other term than heartsick, and he despised himself for it. Brilliant as he was, there was obviously something wrong with him if he could be so obsessed with something he had made from scratch yet spinelessly allow it to walk out on him.

He went to bed with Janet every Friday night after a restaurant dinner and a movie either in a theater or on DVD, and then often enough put another, an oldie, on television while they had sex and looked at it intermittently. They were thoroughly comfortable with each other by now, so much so that they rarely conversed.

4

When first on her own Phyllis had no address. She could not use most of what was offered by an abode. She did not eat, sleep, or require a bathroom. Heating and air conditioning were personally meaningless to her.

To charge her batteries a source of electrical power was necessary periodically. She used the 110-volt outlets provided at public-library tables for laptops needing a boost, where the other patrons were scholarly solipsists.

She spent a good deal of time at libraries, doing research into show business, in trade papers or on the internet. She learned that even to get a toe in the door could not be done without acquiring an agent, but little was more difficult than persuading one to sign you on unless you already had some work, which situation was another of the apparent absurdities in human affairs.

But before looking for an agent, she had to establish a reliable means by which he could get in touch with her if he found her a job. Having no home and lacking the money with which even to rent a room, she had no telephone.

At first a public phone on a street corner seemed to be the answer, but in choosing the right one she attracted the interest of some other women walking nearby. They were prostitutes. As soon as they determined that Phyllis was not the competition, they became friendly with her and, illogically, invited her into their ranks, another of the absurdities almost routine when trafficking with human beings.

At the outset, Phyllis thought practicing this profession temporarily might provide her with an income with which to acquire a domicile where she could have a telephone. As a whore she would have certain strengths peculiar to a nonhuman: immunity to disease or pregnancy, tirelessness, and a constitutional incapacity to be offended physically, emotionally, or morally by any demand.

But it turned out that streetwalkers were handled by agents known as pimps, who wore elaborate clothing and cruised in gaudy cars, and according to the working girls to whom Phyllis spoke, commandeered the moneys so earned, returning to them only meager allowances.

This arrangement, which made no sense to Phyllis, because the pimp brought them no customers, all of whom the girls hustled themselves, was however perfectly agreeable to the hookers who were her informants. "He really love us bitches," said Lily, six feet tall counting the height of the red wig, to which Ashley, shivering in her skimpy satin teddy on a 40-degree night, added, "And we motherfucking love that daddy. It's a family, Phyl, you know what I'm sayin'?"

But Phyllis could see no advantage for herself in this calling. She also learned that selling one's body for sexual purposes was illegal though lending it for free was not. Human beings could also legally sell their own blood.

Ashley did make one suggestion that seemed viable, namely, that Phyllis might want to try her luck at a strip club with what looked like a good body that hopefully, unlike Ashley's own, was unscarred by surgery done by butchers and free of the track marks conspicuous on Lily's skin-and-bone forearms.

"Nice tits. Now drop your drawers," said Eddie, a balding man wearing a dark suit over a black T-shirt, behind a desk in the office of a club called Flashes.

Phyllis removed her underpants. Eddie's office had dark-green walls on which photographs of naked female performers were displayed, along with a calendar, advertising a firm called Currier & Ives, which bore a picture of persons of a bygone age about to enter a vehicle to which a team of four-footed, long-legged animals was hitched. No doubt there was an explanation for this picture. Phyllis was at her greatest disadvantage when asked to deal with the past, having so brief a one of her own.

"Great ass," said Eddie, indicating, with a revolving motion of a hairy crooked finger, that she should turn. "Know what I like about your bush is you don't have a bikini burn." He made a shrug that involved his thick neck and shadowy chin. "Phyllis, is it? Okay, Phyl, you can go on soon as you get an outfit, which you pay for. Understand, no money ever goes from the club to you. The girls are all amateurs, not employees. You don't get no benefits—health, vacations, that shit. But you keep all tips, and they are up to you so long as you don't break the law, which is you can't touch a guy's cock with your hands and he can't touch your tits or pussy with his. Between sets you go into the audience and do lap dances, rub your lower body against his clothed crotch, but he can't expose his dick."

"I am stripped completely nude?"

"That's right, you're naked but he ain't. Also, you can't jerk him off with your hand but you can get him off with your ass. Makes sense to the lawmakers, I guess, and undercover cops come in from time to time to check. We generally recognize them, but we got to be careful because at this time they're not on the take and could bust you and close us down. . . . It's risky to make dates to meet off the premises if money's involved. You could be charged with prostitution."

"The club makes its income from the cover charge and the drinks?" Phyllis had observed that financial matters ranked among the most important in human connections, probably because they were easier than emotions and morality to quantify.

"You got it," said Eddie. He opened a desk drawer and groped within, at last finding and passing on to Phyllis a little printed card. "Where our girls get their stage outfits. Give 'em this and get ten percent discount. Now the only thing left to know is you don't have to blow the bouncers for free, irregardless of what they tell you. They bother you too much for sexual favors, just let me know. As for me, that's my old lady who's the cashier. Nuff said?" He showed very white teeth in a probable smile.

The performer did not simply take off her clothes when she came onto the stage at the far end of the club. While slowly stripping, the removal of each garment taking as much as a minute, she danced to the loud music that came over the public-address system. For some this had a fast tempo and spirited rhythms, but other girls moved to slower, more measured accompaniment. When asked her preference, Phyllis had not had any. She could not understand why men who wanted to look at naked women needed all the unnecessary hocus-pocus attending what should have been the simplest of events.

Also, she had never danced and had difficulty in making order of what she saw the other girls doing, most of which motions seemed to have no organic relation to those used in walking. The music, of whichever sort, was more hindrance than help.

Phyllis had to get a loan from a reluctant Eddie to buy a costume at the fancy-underwear shop he recommended, two doors from the club: fishnet stockings supported by a black-lace garter belt under which was a black satin cache-sexe, the strings of which converged into one in the furrow between her buttocks. Above the waist she wore a filmy bra through which her breasts were visible but could be made even more conspicuous by folding back little panels that covered the apertures through which her nipples protruded. Though the dancer was almost bare to begin with, the prevailing style was deliberately to remove garment by garment, taking much more time than should have been needed to undress, but as Phyllis observed, it apparently did not annoy the audience of men, which began with those seated immediately around the U-shaped stage, the floor of which was low enough for them to lean their forearms on it, with fists clutching paper money. From time to time the performer would crouch before a man waving a bill and rapidly thrust her pelvis toward him, withdrawing it as quickly. On average she repeated the movement thrice before leaving her groin in the extended position until he inserted the bill behind the patch of satin concealing her genital organ—without, according to Eddie, touching the flesh with anything but the money, on pain of violating the law and being expelled by the bouncers.

Phyllis had carefully observed the girls who performed before her, and when it was her own turn to go on she made an initial effort to imitate them, but could not quickly catch on to dancing, which, if she tried too strenuously, threatened to take her back to the early days when Ellery was training her to walk, when she had often fallen to the ground. Who would repair her if she damaged herself now? So she confined her movements to a vigorous stride around the U, undressing as she went, and when nude she knelt before the nearest man brandishing a greenback.

He wore eyeglasses and graying sideburns. His nose was sharp with exasperation. "Where am I supposed to put it?"

Phyllis relieved him of the problem by taking the bill with her fingers.

After she had done the same with two more customers, Eddie looked out from backstage and gestured for her to come to him. "Listen, Phyl, you ain't makin' it. Go out and do some lap dances instead." He told her to collect her garments and put them on. "You can sit facing the customer with your legs spread and rub your titties in his face, or you can spread *his* legs and get inside them and rub your crotch against his dick. Or you can turn and sit down facing away and grind your ass into him. Collect the tips soon as you sit down, and then get some more from him if you stay more'n three minutes. Don't quote a price, but you don't have to accept less than you want. Also remind him he's got to buy a drink every ten minutes. The waiters are the bouncers, and vice versa." He smiled at her. "You never done any of this before, have you? What are you, some college student? I never asked for ID, was I wrong?"

"I'm not legally underage."

Eddie chuckled. "Know how I knew that? I can tell a girl's

age within two years by one look at her snatch." He raised his eyebrows. "I mean it. I seen so many!"

Phyllis made her way as far from the stage as possible, suspecting that the customers who sat at tables in the twilit rear might constitute a better market than those closer to the dancers, who would be more interested in looking. A burly bouncer-waiter had just placed a bottle of beer in front of a frail-looking little fellow in a suit jacket that rose up and away from the back of his collar.

"*Twenty* dollars? Twenty for a bottle of domestic beer?"

The waiter pointed with a carrot-sized finger. "Get the fuck out."

"I'll pay," the little man said. "But I can complain, can't I?"

The waiter seized the extended bill. "No!" He lumbered away.

"How do you like that?" the man said to Phyllis. "I don't know why they have to be nasty in places that have to do with sex."

"I think it's because these places are somewhat degrading. Many of the clients would not like it widely known that they come here, the married ones for obvious reasons, and even the single men would probably want to be discreet about it, because people might get the idea that they are incapable of normal sexual relations. So those who run these establishments feel superior to their clientele."

"Are you the house philosopher?" the man asked. He pushed his chair away from the table and patted his narrow lap. "Put it right there." She stayed where she was. "Oh, that's right," said he, producing a bill that even in the dim light Phyllis could see was a ten. But two of those she had collected on stage had been tens. Surely a lap dance was worth more.

"How much do you want, then?" the man asked.

"I'm not a prostitute."

When he held out another ten, she sat down on him and brought her clothed breasts against his face. He pushed her far enough back to converse and, though the nearby tables were empty, spoke in an undertone. "I'll pay another twenty if you slip your hand into my fly and jack me off."

"That's against the law," said Phyllis.

"Only you and me will know."

"Do you want me to grind my behind into your groin?"

"Let's go somewhere private and you give me head. It's worth fifty to me."

"The rubbing with front or back is the only thing that's allowed here."

"Why?"

"It's the law," said Phyllis. "As you know very well. You're an undercover policeman."

"You're nuts."

Her hasty departure from the man's lap brought the waiter-bouncer. "Your ass is grass, pal."

"Step back, bonehead," said the smaller man, rising from the chair with a badge in his hand.

"Yes, sir. You bet." The bouncer rapidly left the neighborhood.

"You lucked out, baby," the detective told Phyllis. "See you around."

"I never break the law if I know what it is," said she. "That's the way I was made." When he was gone she counted her money and, finding she had accumulated fifty dollars, found Eddie in his office.

"You're quitting already?"

"This is really not for me. It might be otherwise if I could dance."

Eddie grinned at her. "There's something different about you, Phyl, though I can't put my finger on it. Listen, you just leave the outfit in the dressing room, and I'll call us even." His grin widened to reveal the tips of his canine teeth. "We own the lawnjeray shop too. I'll keep the fifty, and you can take the g-string with you." He was of course not aware that she was incapable of soiling any intimate garment, nor did she perspire. He accepted the money, though not without counting it. "So, whatya going to do now, Phyl?"

"Try to get into show business."

He rubbed the lobe of his nose, fingertip not quite penetrating the nostril. "Here's something you might consider. My brother Larry's got a phone-sex business. Can you talk filthy?"

"I'm sure I can if I'm told how."

Eddie's eyebrows rose and fell. "I always thought that was instinct. Discuss it with Larry. You'll be wasting your good looks. Most of the women he hires are dogs. It doesn't matter, because nobody sees them. But you're a finicky kind, and hell, you won't get your hands dirty."

Larry did not physically resemble Eddie, being tall, thin, and fair-complexioned, but Phyllis could see no reason to doubt the latter's statement that they were brothers. Blood relationships were difficult for her to understand, having no blood.

"It's not just using profanity," Larry told her. "Some fellows get turned off by raw talk and want something softer, you know. Play it by ear. Ten dollars a minute, the slower the better. Stretch it out. The whole idea is suspense. Just remember it's all over once they come, so it's the reverse of what a hooker does, who gets a guy off as soon as possible, because she's already collected all the money she's likely to get." He frowned and asked, "Why's somebody looks like you want to work a phone? You ain't gonna make anywhere near what you could get selling tail." He immediately answered his own question. "Well, you got your reasons."

Phyllis had already learned that if you didn't volunteer information about yourself, you probably wouldn't be asked by people in the sex industry. Larry said he paid a girl ten percent of what a caller was charged, which averaged out at around fifty dollars per five minutes, and you could talk a good fifty minutes out of every hour. You could take a break occasionally, go to the toilet or drink something if your throat got dry. You could stay on shift as long as you wanted, but most of his employees did only the four-hour minimum, because they had families to get home to, and anyway there weren't many who could talk continuously—or in fact listen—much longer than that at one stretch.

The job sounded ideal to Phyllis, who, as long as her batteries were charged, needed no breaks whatsoever and, having no other life, could work interminably. Though perhaps not exactly show business, it was a close relative, calling as it did for acting at least with the voice.

The phone-sex shop consisted of a half-dozen shallow cubicles of unpainted plywood, each furnished with a little table that held a telephone, a stopwatch, and a bottle of water. At every table but one sat a "hostess" wearing a headset, and as Larry led Phyllis to the unoccupied booth, all of them were speaking into their respective mouthpieces. Two, spotting her out of the corners of their eyes, waved amiably.

All these women appeared to be of another kind than either the streetwalkers or the strippers, being overweight with irregular features and dressed for comfort and not for the enticement of men. By what seemed to be human standards, none could be considered young, though Phyllis had no training and little experience in assessing age numerically and was herself, so far as that went, less than a year old.

When a call came in, the customer was first greeted automatically by an introductory message on audio tape announcing, quickly and not at all clearly, the fees for which he would be responsible if he stayed on the line after the introduction was concluded and he had stated his credit-card number and expiration date. He was then transferred to whichever woman whose line was open. If all the phones were in use, he was put on hold, for which time he was assured he would not be charged, but this was one of the several lies that Larry usually got away with. Few callers actually timed themselves precisely, and the waits were not often very long, for contrary to Larry's projection, business was not always so brisk that one could earn the fifty dollars per hour of his estimate.

There were periods in which as few as two lines were in use. After her first three hours, Phyllis estimated her take at only forty dollars, at a rate of $13.33 per hour.

At off times, the idle women by turns visited the restroom. Having no reason to do so, Phyllis did not go there until her nearest neighbor praised her endurance.

"If I could hold it, I sure would. The last time that place was cleaned will be the first," said the woman, whose name was May Bellaver. May had been married for twenty-three years to a man who drove a machine called a backloader for some county department. She had borne three children, of whom the oldest was a college dropout who played guitar in a band that rarely found gigs; the youngest, a girl who had just got her period; and in between a male child of fifteen whom she suspected of computer hacking, though it was too complicated for her to figure out. The husband's position regarding the kids had always been hands off. "Sports," she added cryptically, and then explained: "All he does when he's home is watch sports."

When Phyllis entered the washroom for the first time she saw what May meant about its lack of cleanliness, and having a few minutes of privacy owing to Larry's rule that only one woman at a time could be away from the phones, she found a mop, a bucket, and other cleaning materials in a closet and quickly washed the floor, Ajaxed the washbasin and faucets, and swabbed out the toilet.

Phyllis would have had no idea of what to say to a caller, but Larry had given her sufficient guidelines to get started, and she learned from every call she took.

"I'm Phyllis. Tell me what I can do for you." She could have used a pseudonym like the others—May's was Felicity—but she had no personal identity to conceal.

"I've been a bad boy, Phyllis," was the way many callers began. "I must be punished. My name is, uh, Paul."

It was not her business to ask what kind of crime could properly be punished by what a stranger said on the telephone. "You deserve no mercy, Paul," she said sternly. "Get your clothes off, you worm."

"I'm naked, Mistress."

"My rawhide whip has been soaking in vinegar. Every time it hits your naked ass, it'll open up a deep cut, and when the vinegar meets a bleeding wound, the pain will be agonizing."

"Ohhhh, do it, Mistress. . . . What about my balls?"

"I'm going to rip them off."

"My God, I'm ready to come right now."

Phyllis was supposed to delay this outcome until the customer had been on the line for at least five minutes, arousing him but then periodically curbing the arousal, but she was by nature, which is to say by design, inclined to a mode of operation unsympathetic to delay. She also found it hard to understand why a man would find so desirable a postponement of his satisfaction that he would pay extra for it.

But customers often wanted her to go into painstaking detail about what she would do with their sexual organs, rectum, mouth, even ears and nostrils. Some might by contrast provide a lengthy account of what they would do with hers. They could not of course be criticized for an ignorance of her material composition. Those who wanted to chew the crotch of her dirty underwear were not aware that it would smell exactly as it had when she put it on.

Now and again someone called who wanted *her* to play the bad child, to speak in a high-pitched voice and in fantasy lie across his naked lap while he lowered her little white cotton panties and spanked her tiny pink butt until *she* was so sexually excited that she would rape *him* by one means or another, which seemed to Phyllis impractical if she were as small as she was supposed to be.

Occasionally she could not forbear from pointing out absurdities in what a customer would say or ask, even though Larry had warned her against negative expression that did not enhance the pleasure of the caller.

For example, you could threaten to do physical harm, castration and other mutilations, flogging, choking, et cetera, but not reflect on the man's taste, judgment, or morality. "Remember, this is all just talk, Phyl. The customer's always right if he keeps paying." Yet when a man told her that what he wanted to hear was the sounds she would make if after buggering her with a Coke bottle he snuffed her with a razor blade across the throat, Phyllis believed she should point out that while such fantasies were not illegal, any attempt to realize them would be against the law.

Comparing notes with May during the periods when neither was on the phone, Phyllis observed that no callers yet had asked to speak about the straightforward sort of intercourse in which the penis is inserted into the vagina and agitated to the point of climax.

May's hearty laughter sent a vibration through her several chins. "You got a good sense of humor, Phyl. You're right about these guys: If they was normal, they wouldn't be calling here. My old man never heard of most of this stuff, I only hope. I never grew up in a convent, but most of it was new to me until I worked the phones, I don't mind telling you." She laughed till she had to dry her eyes on a Kleenex. "If you took it serious, you'd go nuts."

"Your husband approves of this job?"

"I tell him it's telemarketing, which I guess it is. He never asked *what* I was telemarketing."

"Sports."

"That's right; he just watches sports. But he likes the money I bring home, damn if he don't."

She added proudly, "I bought him a wide-screen TV." She took a swig from her water bottle. "Excuse me asking, Phyl. You ever been married?"

"I'm separated."

May's phone rang at that point, and a second later, so did Phyllis's.

"I got ten inches at full erection," said her caller, "and a great big pair of hairy balls. I want you to crawl across the floor on your naked belly, and when you get here rise to your knees and pray to this majestic god that looms above you, beg his forgiveness for your sins, swear your absolute loyalty to him, for which you may be asked the ultimate sacrifice, hail his grandeur, salute his glory—are you listening, you piece of nothing, to the mighty voice of King Cock?"

"Yes," said Phyllis.

"Well, what are you going to do about it?"

"Everything you mentioned."

"Not enough. I'm paying for this!"

"What else do you want?"

"You tell *me*, for Christ sake."

"I just wish I knew," Phyllis said. "What can be done for the man who already has everything?"

Larry appeared suddenly and took the phone from her. Into it he said, "I'm sorry, sir, your call got mistakenly switched to the wrong extension. Let me correct this."

"I'm not being charged for this, I hope."

"No, sir," Larry lied. "First minute's free. Hold on." To Phyllis he said, with crooked finger, "C'mon. Listen to this."

She left her cubicle and, passing four others with hostesses on the phone, followed him to the last, the left-side partition of which was the wall. This was occupied by a woman who was doing the crossword puzzle in a magazine. She appeared to be the oldest of the lot, with completely white hair, crow's-footed eyes, and withered cheeks. She squinted up at Larry through the top lenses of bifocal glasses.

"Liz, pick up Five."

The old woman nodded briskly, punched the appropriate

button, and lifted the telephone. Her voice was a surprise to Phyllis, being so much younger-sounding than she looked. "Master, Desirée at your service. . . . Oh, it's the most magnificent I've ever seen. I live only to worship and adore it. . . . Yes, oh please, please, *please* do not deny me. I want only to serve it. . . ."

After a few moments of this, Larry drew Phyllis aside. "S'why I been monitoring your calls, Phyl. You got to develop some patience. Maybe that's because you're too good-looking for this job. You're wasting it, is what you're doing. Them others here, this is the best they can do."

"I'm really trying to get into show business."

"Eddie tells me it didn't work out forya at the club," said Larry. "Listen, I got an idea. C'mon in the office, talk it over."

His office was much more sparsely furnished than his brother Eddie's, with unpainted plywood walls like those of the cubicles, a table made from a flat door resting on sawhorses, atop which were a laptop computer and a telephone. He gestured Phyllis to a folding metal chair and, behind the table, took another for himself.

"In my opinion, the best opportunities for a hot girl in the sex business these days is websites." He threw a thumb at the open laptop. "According to Eddie, you had some difficulty in relating to the live audience. Well, it isn't for everybody. Neither is phones. But on the internet, you got a variety to choose from. What I think might work for you is a voyeur site. Now, you got different kinds of them, too. You got your houses where a number of girls go about their business twenty-four/seven while cameras watch everything they do, undressing, showering, the toilet included, and everything in the bedrooms including blowing and fucking their boyfriends." Larry smiled abstractly, looking just past Phyllis. "Just living, not acting. And then there's the individual sites: One girl performs for the camera, you know? Plays with her titties and cooze, talks dirty, uses a dildo, and so on, and will do requests by e-mail. She doesn't see them, so it's personal for them but not her. That might be the ticket for you, Phyl. Takes some acting ability. Fingering your pussy over and over again for hours is, once again, not for every girl, and then there's the audio: You got to keep ad-libbing, like on the phones."

"I'd be willing to try it," said Phyllis.

"Great." Larry pulled the laptop in front of him and began to press its keys. "This is how me and my brother communicate nowadays."

"Your brother Eddie?"

He looked at her over the machine. "My brother Harry. He's right downstairs in this building. We got the two floors." He leaned forward to peer at the screen. "Harry says . . . come right down." Larry pushed his chair away from the table.

"Thank you," said Phyllis. "I believe I have fifty-five dollars coming for the four hours I worked the phone."

Larry returned to the computer and manipulated the keys. "Okay, Phyl, here's how it looks. During the training period you get only five percent, which I think you'll agree is generous in view of that last call which you bungled. There's a slight charge for the bottled water."

"Which I didn't touch."

Larry ignored her comment and consulted the screen again. "You've got thirty bucks coming, but I have to owe it to you till the end of the month. I don't get paid for the calls till the credit-card companies pay me." He pushed his chair back again and spread his legs. "You owe *me* for sending you to Harry. If you want to go down on me as a thank-you, I might find a few extra dollars."

Phyllis still had two-thirds of her last charge, and her coordination was not disordered as it had been the night she went temporarily haywire and tried to punch Ellery Pierce. Rational now, she stood up, went to Larry, and knocked him out with one blow to a chin made prominent by a triumphant smirk. She found a leather wallet in the breast pocket of his jacket. From its abundant supply of bills she extracted a twenty and a ten.

As she returned the wallet to his pocket, Larry groaned and without opening his eyes murmured, "You can't kill a man for tryin'."

The statement made no sense to Phyllis, but then thus far very little had in the area of human morality. In her opinion, people should stick to what they did well, namely, technology.

5

Before long, Ellery Pierce and Janet Hallstrom were so comfortable with each other as no longer to be sexually intimate, and since they did not live together, there seemed little point in maintaining their connection. Soon he saw her, often with Hallstrom, only by chance, at the entrance to the apartment building or in the hallway, and though it could well be only because he knew the latter for an animatronic creature, Pierce no longer found it or him altogether credible. The old sparkle in the eye of apparent vitality, though of course always simulated, was missing now. Hallstrom's responses seemed diminished from what they had been. He no longer initiated the banal polite conversations of old, the platitudes about the weather, the clichés on the traffic problem, and other minutiae of quotidian life. Whether he was still being nasty to Janet could not be discerned from the countenance of either.

For his own part, Pierce failed to feel the least sensitivity, on seeing Hallstrom, that he normally would have known in the presence of a human husband whom he had cuckolded. But as time went by he felt more and more as though he had been rejected in a human way by Phyllis's departure. The difference was that as his creation she could not be altogether a machine. Her moral status would properly be at the level of daughter or wife, while being neither. Their special relationship might not be what had hitherto been included under the umbrella of normality, but he was no more a pervert than Phyllis was a sex doll.

Something unique had occurred in the process of her making, something that had escaped his attention at the time, but perusing the copious notes he had kept did him no good now in his efforts to produce her successor, which had thus far failed in almost every particular. Though the advances in technology since he had first begun to construct Phyllis I should have made the job with II easier at almost every stage, he kept encountering new obstacles. The latest development in artificial flesh, which could be brought more quickly to normal human body temperature and maintained there with an improved thermostat, did not have, to Pierce's touch, quite the old resilience . . . that was to say, Phyllis's.

Try as he did with every supplier, he simply could not find the perfect hazel of artificial eye—the hazel of Phyllis's. He paid a fortune for a vast selection of human hair from various European sources without acquiring a match for that on Phyllis's scalp, which was finer, silkier, more richly yet subtly colored, though itself synthetic—he had previously exhausted the capabilities of all those who produced the latter.

As to a voice, every version was impossible, erring someplace across a range from oleaginous to abrasive. Any attempt to soften coarseness of timbre resulted in a creamy loss of character. Concentrating for months on one sound, that of his own name—Phyllis's pronunciation of which he cherished above all others, and which he had invoked from her almost immediately—he could now reproduce nothing that came close to her perfect pitch, her elegant but never pretentious enunciation, the flutelike tones of glee, the cello of passion.

Phyllis's had been a miraculous conception, not the sort of thing that one could reasonably expect to be repeated. The longer she was gone, the more mythic she became to Pierce, who was in danger of losing a clear image of her in a general refulgence, which state of affairs he believed deplorable but also remarkable, given his basic irreligiosity.

Lack of success in creating another artificial woman had its effect on his professional career. While previously moonlighting on Phyllis's construction, often being distracted by it and in fact stealing the materials from which she was made, he had nevertheless done such outstanding work on his firm's projects that he had been appointed head of the research department of Animatronics, Inc. But now, having arrived at an impasse in the effort to build her successor, Pierce neglected his job, his attention turning diffuse in matters that demanded precision, his focus no nearer than the middle distance. Seeking to conceal the void in his moral authority, he assumed a brusque style that appeared rude to his colleagues, who rather sooner than later were turned against him by his second-in-command and hitherto secret rival when, failing to see the extraordinary potential in the new and revolutionary miniature power source—a kerosene-fueled turbine the size of a postage stamp—Pierce rejected an opportunity to acquire it exclusively.

Unemployed for the first time in two decades, not indigent but obliged by signed severance agreement not to work for a competitor for one year, in exchange for a sum of money on which to exist in the interim, Pierce disintegrated further in spirit. Never having replaced the cleaning woman whom Phyllis had discharged, he lived among disorder and, in the kitchen, worse. Dirty underwear and socks were strewn from room to room. He padded about barefoot, with filthy soles, until pricking a toe on an open safety pin he had lost when, all drunken thumbs, he tried to tighten the elastic of the pajama bottom that was now too loose owing to the decline in weight resulting from a loss of appetite. Phyllis's cooking had ruined his palate for all other fare.

From the "gimlets" he drank nowadays all but the gin was eliminated, and when the gin ran out he started in on the vodka purchased for the fateful dinner party, an all but tasteless liquid he had formerly disdained but now found as good an anesthetic as any, which was to say, not very, and his doctor refused to write him a prescription for anything actually effective at relieving effects of emotional deprivation and mental distress. Pierce could not bring himself to confess even to a physician that he was in such a state because he had been abandoned by a device he had built with his own hands—and heart.

6

Harry, who resembled neither of the two brothers Phyllis had met, was a very fat man, the excess flesh of whose face diminished his eyes and mouth, which likely were of normal size. His voice was deep and resonant.

"Very well, put your clothes on," said he from the wheelchair in which he had come to view her at close range. The chair was, like Phyllis, powered by storage battery. Harry sent it rolling back behind the desk and asked, "Do you do anal?"

"I'm not sure." She buttoned her blouse.

"How can't you know if you take it up the ass or not?" Harry asked genially. "That's not subject to much interpretation."

Incapable of coyness, Phyllis had answered literally. Ellery had not provided her with a colon, which would have had no natural function. She was not sure as to the proportions of her rectal aperture.

"Unless," Harry went on in the same amiable tone, "you mean no, and it's okay if you do. We don't use duress around here. The purpose of sex is pleasure. Therefore it should be associated with nothing that brings displeasure to anyone"—his smile was so lavish that his features vanished completely— "except prudes." His eyes appeared, and then his lips. "I have a number of websites, embracing a diversity of pleasures. Do you have any preferences?"

"I want to get into show business," Phyllis said. She knew that might sound simplistic, but she could not come up with a better statement of her aim. She believed that if she specified only one area, say movies, it might be thought she was excluding TV, and so on.

"You've come to the right place," said Harry, his voice growing ever more jovial. "Would you happen to know *Hamlet*, Phyllis?"

"A town?"

"A play by Shakespeare, in which one of the characters speaks about show business: 'pastoral-comical, historical-pastoral, tragical-historical,' et cetera." Harry paused to jiggle with laughter. "At Sexsites Unlimited we offer all combinations: oral-anal, anal-fecal, urino-oral, gerio-masochist—"

"What's that last?" Phyllis asked.

Harry beamed. "Pubescent girls try to stimulate senile men. According to our e-mail, most who log on to that are women in middle age."

"Is it not a violation of the law for underaged persons to participate in the performance of sexual acts?"

Harry briefly became solemn. "That's why we use short, slightly built women with shaved pudenda. They've proved much more credible than computer-generated figures." His eyes vanished again, but only for an instant, then reappeared wide open. "You'll find nothing illegal here, Officer."

"I'm not an undercover cop," said Phyllis.

"All right," Harry said. "But there's something different about you that I can't put a finger on." He winked. "And don't worry that I'll try. I'm totally gay. Now bring a chair around here and take a look at what we offer." He gestured at the large monitor on the desk.

Phyllis did as asked. Harry logged on to a succession of websites, each of which was devoted to a particular type of sexual activity, justifying the comment he had made for which he used Shakespeare as a reference.

"Not everything," said he, "is for everybody. One person's pleasure might be repulsive to another. You strike me as a genteel sort of woman. I can relate to that. I'm the educated member of the family." Harry found a handkerchief somewhere on his massive person and blotted his expanse of forehead. He was sweating, an effect that Phyllis did not understand, because she could not have produced it herself. A human being was essentially a vessel containing an almost endless variety of fluids.

He turned his head toward her. "I mention Shakespeare because I played Falstaff in a college production. I too felt the lure of the performing arts." He returned to the screen and clicked the mouse. "Aha, now here's something that might appeal. These girls go about their normal daily lives while the cameras run."

"That woman's just examining her face in the bathroom mirror."

"She's about to use the toilet." Harry nodded, his first chin being, so to speak, accordioned into those beneath. "Our subscribers can't get enough of that."

Urine apparently had its devotees. At one of the other sites, a young woman was squatting above a recumbent man, micturating into his face. These people were not acting, but Phyllis would be if she simulated the evacuation of wastes. However, she could do little of the kind without revealing, to the production staff anyway, that she did not consist of flesh and blood, and keeping such a secret seemed imperative, convinced as she was that a nonhuman performer who came out of the closet would not succeed with an audience that craved identification with those who imitated its members.

"I'll tell you, Harry," she said. "I really don't see anything that would be right for me, and I wouldn't want to get side-tracked again. It would be a waste of time for all concerned."

Harry looked kindly at her. "It might surprise you to hear that I understand perfectly. You're looking for a challenge. I was like that myself at your age. Unfortunately I did not stick with my dream. I commend you for holding on to yours. I'm going to send you to a personal friend of mine who produces movies. I can't promise anything, mind you, but at least this will get you in the door." He took a sheet of paper from a drawer in the desk and scrawled several lines of bold black script on it with a felt-tipped pen. He folded the note and sealed it inside an elongated envelope on which he inscribed a name and address.

Phyllis could not feel gratitude, but she was aware that courtesy and graciousness lubricated the social mechanism, and she thanked Harry. "Is this man another of your brothers?"

Harry smiled. "He's no relation. I wouldn't be sending you to him if I didn't feel you have a certain potential distinguishing you from the herd."

Phyllis used a public library computer to discover that William Shakespeare was the greatest writer of all time in the English language. Having no formal education, she suffered from great deficiencies. She realized that up to now her efforts to get into show business had been naïve, her credentials nonexistent. No wonder her only opportunities had been to perform simple-minded functions; she was equipped for nothing better.

She therefore postponed her visit to the movie producer until the following day, so she could meanwhile read the collected works of Shakespeare, a task that took twice as long as the hour she had projected, for the archaic language took a while to comprehend, utilizing the copious footnotes and abundant glossary in the edition she had chosen. In the course of her reading of *Hamlet,* she encountered the passage referred to by Harry, in the lines of a character named Polonius, who was very foolish, but no more so than Hamlet himself, who by his ineffectuality wreaked general havoc on foes and friends, including a mentally retarded female by the name of Ophelia, to play whom convincingly Phyllis would have to suppress any evidence of intelligence.

But that was acting, representing that which might be otherwise in reality. At bottom, like all else created by humanity, it was simple despite appearing superficially complex.

Phyllis still had no home. In the time between the closing of the library in the early evening and whenever the movie studio opened next day, she as usual frequented the venues that stayed open all night and did not require anything of their visitors: airport lounges, hotel lobbies, laundromats, and 24/7 supermarkets, though she was at pains not to attract attention as a potential terrorist at the first named or as a likely prostitute at hotels.

As she needed no sleep or any repose whatever, so long as her batteries retained a charge, Phyllis was hyper-alert and continued to acquire and record information from a multitude of sources. On the other hand, she could collect only what was within a relatively narrow focus. In the expanse of what existed there were many things of which she remained utterly ignorant. Her strength was in trees, not forests, her memory bank containing much that would be of little use—such as the twenty-seven different combinations of brand names and types of tinned tomatoes, crushed, diced, pureed, domestic or foreign, et cetera—unless she were to get a job as a canned-vegetable buyer.

At airports she studied not only the luggage but also the clothing of travelers. As to where they were going, having a clear sense of only the here and now, she was incurious.

Tonight, the first time she had had any money since leaving Ellery to go on her own, Phyllis went to a laundromat, where she put her pants suit through the dry-cleaning machine, one piece at a time, covering her legs with the jacket while the pants were in. After the jacket was clean, she wore it while running the blouse through the washer and dryer. She also washed her underwear though it was not dirty.

Her shoes, stylishly fragile to begin with, showed the effects of having walked everywhere she went for several days, but she could not afford to replace them, judging from the prices posted in show windows. By the time she reached the movie studio, a one-story building smaller than expected and marked with a sign identifying it only as *To the Max Enterprises*, both soles were worn through to the pavement in small, oval apertures at the ball of the foot.

"Oh, yes," said the young man, hardly more than a boy, judging from the quality of the skin around his eyes. He had opened and read Harry's note, sitting behind a desk in the best-looking office Phyllis had yet seen except on TV: wood and leather and brass, and shelves full of multicolored book spines.

"I'll strip," said she.

He put up a small hand. "We'll get to that later. First we'll talk and see if our concepts jibe. Can I offer you a cup of *tisane*? Water? Juice?" When she declined he went on. "I'm Max. Harry doesn't mention your name."

"Phyllis Pierce."

Max nodded briskly with his little chin and large forehead, above which was an abundance of dark hair. "I'm casting for my most ambitious project to date: *Othello*. Are you familiar with the property?"

"By William Shakespeare?"

He blinked his eyes at her. "You do know it. What are your feelings about Desdemona?"

"She's the victim of everybody."

Max frowned and lowered his head for a moment, then came up with a radiant smile. "I think you've got it. By George, you've got it." Phyllis had no idea of why he had suddenly acquired an odd accent, which however he immediately lost, to say, "I'm already picking up new perspectives. Now tell me this: What about race? Do you have any feelings about working with an individual of another color?"

"No."

"You might change your mind when you see his schlong." Max made a fist while grabbing that forearm at the elbow with his free hand. "He's hung like a camel."

"Could that be a sexual innuendo?" Phyllis asked.

Max rolled his eyes and stuck out a thick tongue.

"There's no explicit sex in *Othello*."

Max tossed his head. "There won't be much else in the erotic version. Viewers get antsy if you don't cut to the chase after only the briefest preliminaries. You haven't worked in the industry before?"

"No."

"Well, you don't seem nervous about it. That's to your credit." He gestured. "Now you can show your goods."

While undressing, Phyllis asked, "Are you going to use the dialogue as written by William Shakespeare?"

Max shook his head. "I don't think there'll be much call for it. I'm keeping the essential plot, though: Iago's got the hots for Othello, so he cooks up this dirty trick to get Desdemona out of the way, but it doesn't work, and the whole thing ends up as a threesome."

"Desdemona isn't killed?"

Max winced. "This isn't a snuff film. By the way, there never has been one, did you know that? Government investigated. That's another urban myth." He left the desk to come closer to Phyllis. "Good titties. Who did them? Ornstein?" He palpated both of her breasts. "He gets top dollar, right? Let's see this ass. . . . Uh-huh, it's choice." He turned her front-first and probed between her thighs with a forefinger. "You're awful tight. This African American's got ten inches, thick as a Louisville Slugger. Speaking of which"—he took one step back and felt his own crotch—"this is giving me wood." He returned to his desk and, on the intercom, addressed the elderly female receptionist who had earlier admitted Phyllis. "Hold all calls, Grandma."

"Is that her nickname?" Phyllis asked.

"She's really my grandmother," said Max. "We're partners. I'm not twenty-one yet and can't sign a contract." He had already stepped out of his trousers. "Come over here."

"I'm not going to have sex with you, Max," Phyllis told him. "And I don't want to play Desdemona in the porn *Othello*."

He pouted briefly. "Why'd you strip, then?"

"I was being professional." Phyllis donned her jacket. "You

might make other movies in the future that are not so silly."

"But this is the big one. If it scores I'll keep making sequels. *What* don't you like? Is it Shakespeare? Is it me?"

As Phyllis went through the reception room on her way out of the building, Max's gray-haired grandmother, looking over the spectacles on the end of her nose, said, "That was a quickie. Good-bye, dear. Take care."

7

Pierce got a phone call from Cliff Pulsifer, a name that he could not place until Cliff apologized for not getting back in touch immediately after the marvelous dinner party at which he had been a guest.

"But Ray and I broke up, which took some getting over."

"Yeah," said Pierce. "Phyllis and I split, too, and I haven't gotten over it."

"I suspected as much," said Cliff, "and thought maybe I could help with some crisis management, having been through the same myself."

"How did you hear about it?"

Cliff took an audible breath. "Tyler Hallstrom and I have been living together for several weeks."

"I'll be damned."

"That's the virtue of an animatron." Cliff spoke on a rising note. "They can be anything you want them to be—but look who I'm telling. You wrote the book on the subject. You made your own."

Pierce felt an access of self-pity. "For all the good it did me. I couldn't keep her."

"You shouldn't be all alone with your problem," Cliff said. "Come to dinner, Friday, and get some moral support. If you don't mind takeout. Ray did the cooking. I can't boil water in a microwave, and neither, it seems, can Tyler."

"I don't know, Cliff . . ."

"Please. Is it true you also lost your job?"

"How do you know *that?*"

Cliff's next surprise was that he provided a female dinner companion for Pierce, who was at first offended that this had been done without his being asked or informed. But in the course of the evening Alicia, a slender fortyish brunette with shadowy eyes, ingratiated herself to Pierce by her calm candor, beginning with an unapologetic opting for a fork over chopsticks when offered a choice. She also differed from Cliff on everything else that was conversationally at issue, often saucily though always agreeably. Not until dessert, which Alicia had brought (the only non-Asian element in the meal), did she reveal that Cliff was her baby brother.

Though Pierce could take or leave dishes prepared with fish sauce and lemongrass, he did very much enjoy good old-fashioned three-flavor ice cream, and the strawberry in this one tasted as if it had had some speaking acquaintance with the real fruit. Furthermore, he enjoyed Alicia's repartee with her brother, which served to humanize Cliff, whom Pierce hadn't known all that well. In his loneliness he even began to project a future in which, pursuing a friendship with Alicia, he acquired an instant family.

But when at the end of the evening she invited herself home with him, her purpose proved to be the crisis management of which Cliff had spoken on the telephone but never approached when face-to-face during the dinner party.

Alicia led him to the sofa and sat down close enough to rub knees. "As a Lesbian," she said, her lush lips in a sententious configuration, "I think I can furnish some help with the woman's point of view. And Phyllis, though not human, *is*, I gather, altogether feminine."

"Whatever she is," Pierce noted coolly, "*I* built her from scratch." He moved so that their legs were no longer in contact.

"Aha," said Alicia with a flutter of eyelash. "Cliff failed to mention that important fact. Typically." She sighed. "Of course, this means she is a *man's* idea of a woman, another thing entirely. I can't be expected to relate to her. She will be utterly different from a real woman. She will define herself by her connection with a man. She will be weak-willed, dependent, gentle, clinging, anxious only to serve, uncertain, devoid of conviction, frightened by challenges . . ."

"You've described Phyllis to a T," Pierce said. "Would you like a drink?" He rose.

Alicia stood up too. "Cliff thought I might help. Sorry I can't." She shrugged. "If you don't mind my saying so, robots creep me out. What Cliff sees in that Tyler Hallstrom is beyond me. He used to get really nice fellows."

Speaking of which, Pierce had all but forgotten about Hallstrom soon after arriving at a dinner party that consisted of but three persons at table, with Tyler serving only as waiter and remaining in the kitchen between courses. He showed no recognition of Pierce. His expression stayed so blank as to suggest that his personality chip was missing.

"I guess what Cliff wants at the moment is a servant," Pierce said. "We all have our own needs."

On the way to the door Alicia shook her head and groaned. "You guys and your machines!"

It occurred to Pierce that perhaps he should abandon the idea of re-creating a Phyllis and instead make a man. True, he had never been sexually attracted to a member of his own sex, but he could use a male pal and, just as Phyllis represented everything he sought in a woman, a handcrafted Philip could be fashioned to play the role of the perfect friend, providing commiseration when Pierce's fortunes ebbed, as now, but cheering when the tide was reversed, for Phil would be innocent of envy. He need not be particularly good-looking, but it might be useful to make him husky, should Pierce be threatened with violence by other human beings, muggers, irrational road-ragers, or truculent drunks at public events. Any damage Phil sustained could be repaired, even gunshot wounds. He could do all the driving, as well, and be programmed to shop for Pierce's clothing, a job Pierce himself had no taste for, and to pick up every check: a convenience, though Pierce would ultimately pay them. If they double-dated, Phil could be counted on not to compete for the attention of the women and to appear somewhat inferior to Pierce in every area, though without being so blatantly obsequious as to arouse suspicion. Finally, Philip would need no genitals—or should Pierce want to work out with his friend at the gym, only a nonusable set for locker-room appearances.

For amusement Pierce projected future episodes in which a gay guy put the moves on Phil in the shower, or a female date's hopes were dashed when Philip showed no reaction to a tongue in his throat. . . . But these were just idle fantasies. Pierce was not motivated by spite. Even when down he refused to put his craft at the service of negation. He would not construct an animatronic man. He would instead search for Phyllis and, finding her, reverse his previous position and demand that she return to him. If this did not work, he would beg and snivel. How could he be degraded by groveling before his own creation? Pride could mean nothing to Phyllis.

8

Phyllis of course never forgot any of her assigned dialogue, or for that matter anyone else's, in what actors, honoring a traditional backstage superstition, called the Scottish Play.

Macbeth was played by a man named Douglas Bigelow. When he forgot a line in any of the scenes they shared, or the prompter cued him in too soft a tone for Doug to hear, for he was a bit deaf, Phyllis delivered his lines.

"What's to be done?" Lady Macbeth would ask in Act III, Scene 2, and if her husband failed to make a timely response, she would answer herself:

> Be innocent of the knowledge, dearest chuck,
> Till thou applaud the deed. Come, seeling night,
> Scarf up the tender eye of pitiful day . . .

Occasionally when so jump-started, Doug would take over on one of her natural pauses for breath (though having no need to breathe, Phyllis simulated doing so to provide the proper rhythm for William Shakespeare's verse) and complete the speech himself. More often, failing to recover, he let her finish all twelve lines that closed the scene, after which he would stagger into the wings and find the pint of vodka he had cached in a firebucket.

Early on, Phyllis had asked Doug why he drank so much, and he said, "I'm scared. Much of the dialogue doesn't make any sense to me, so I forget it. I joined this group to do modern things, *Streetcar*, *Death of a Salesman*. Howard talked me into Shakespeare. Next he wants to do *Medea*."

"I thought I knew everything William Shakespeare wrote," said Phyllis, "including even *The Two Noble Kinsmen*, which many scholars don't believe was his, except for a few lines."

"*Medea*'s Greek tragedy," said Bigelow. "In revenge against her husband, the title character cooks her own children and serves them to him for dinner. Sick stuff. . . . I can sing, you know. I'd like to do Rodgers and Hammerstein."

When Phyllis told Doug's troubles to Howard Kidd, the director and founder of the suburban theater company, he shrugged his narrow shoulders.

"So he goes up in his lines, like everybody does from time to time except you, Phyl. So what? The audience never knows. They don't understand any more of the text than he does."

Before getting her big break, Phyllis had begun as flunky and gofer for Kidd, whose little theater was a personal project funded by himself, or rather by his rich wife. The unpaid casts were made up of amateurs who loved to perform. Doug Bigelow, for example, sold computers; Jane Wilhelm, Phyllis's predecessor as Lady Macbeth, taught high school English. The roster of nonperforming personnel, backstage and box office, tended frequently to change from weekend to weekend. Even though the theater was open only on Friday and Saturday evenings during short spring and fall seasons, there was a great deal of exhausting work to be done for no tangible reward but a listing of names in the xeroxed program.

Kidd had readily accepted Phyllis as an unpaid apprentice, and in that job she painted, hauled, and erected scenery, and, after a bit of research, did carpentry as well. She mounted posters, wherever such were permitted, all over town and several nearby villages. She handled the accounts for the theater, as well as Kidd's correspondence. She served as property manager and wardrobe mistress, stage manager and prompter. Once, when Kidd was down with the flu, she assumed directorial authority and forced what she recognized as a cast grown stale in their roles to rehearse and crisp up some of the performances, for example that of the retired postman named Ned Stilling, whose Banquo was overly decrepit. In so doing, Phyllis offended these people, who after all were not professionals and performed for audiences that, after the openings in which most of the seventy-five seats would be filled with relatives and friends, in the later days of the run might number fewer than half a dozen.

But as soon as Kidd had returned and Phyllis had gone back to her normal functions she was quickly forgiven by all, owing to the unfailing good humor and tireless energy with which she did everything that looked like labor, freeing the actors to dwell on the artistic plane.

Kidd himself was less appreciative. The more tasks Phyllis took on, the more critical of her he became. Before her arrival, the cleaning of the theater had been done on the morning before each performance by a volunteer crew of high school students under the supervision of Jane Wilhelm, their moonlighting teacher. They did a negligent job even early in the engagement, and by the third weekend most of them failed to appear, but Phyllis easily fitted this chore into her schedule, making short work of sweeping the little theater, mopping the lavatories, and polishing the metal fixtures and glass.

Some of the folding camp chairs that accommodated the audience were the worse for years of wear. Phyllis tightened their connections and revarnished many, early enough in the week so that all tackiness would have dried by Friday. On an extension ladder, she confirmed her suspicion that the house lights wore filters of grime and cleaned them thoroughly.

Kidd was not impressed. "You piss your time away on make-work when what I need is audience."

"The difficulty," she pointed out, "is that the nearby population is not large enough to sustain even a small theater devoted to classics performed in the time-honored way."

"I hope you're not about to suggest a *Hamlet* with a circus theme—Horatio dressed as a clown, Ophelia playing an aerialist. I *loathe* modernizations of Shakespeare." He brandished a fist at the ceiling. "I'd rather go dark for good, and I may have to." He made a noise between a grunt and a gasp. Human beings could produce at will compromises of sound beyond Phyllis's capacity. "The latest news is that my wife is definitely pulling out her support from under me. I made the point that just because she hates my guts and is terminating the marriage, it shouldn't have a necessary bearing on the fate of the theater, but she didn't buy it. She might have if her lawyer were not such a nasty motherfucker. First kill all the lawyers!"

"'The first thing we do, let's kill all the lawyers,'" Phyllis quoted correctly. "Dick the Butcher, *Henry the Sixth, Part Two*, Act Four, Scene Two, line twenty-seven."

"She was crazy about me once," said Kidd. "She bought me

off. I might have gone somewhere on Broadway. This little theater was a consolation prize."

"Have you ever appeared in any of the productions here?"

"Who wouldn't rather direct than let somebody else run him
around?"

"Acting is a magical art," Phyllis said.

"You say that only because you haven't done any."

"By the way, Jane is giving notice."

"Oh, shit!" Kidd howled. "Can't you talk her into staying?
There's only next weekend left."

"Her husband's going into the hospital for a double bypass."

"That's bullshit. Can't he wait? Or can't she just come here
for a couple hours, two nights? As a personal favor to me, who
she owes so much?"

"She doesn't wish you well, Howard. She says you're lucky
she didn't go to the police when she caught you putting the
moves on her fifteen-year-old."

Kidd lifted a trio of fingers and lowered them one by one as
he made the respective assertions. "Three things. One, she's
lying. Two, what steamed that ugly little bitch was I *didn't* come
on to her. Three, the lying slut swore she was twenty-one while
zipping open my fly with her teeth."

Kidd's wife was divorcing him because of his taste for adoles-
cents, to whom he promised parts that were never forthcoming.
It was convenient for Phyllis to look too old for him.

"*I* want to play Lady Macbeth next Friday and Saturday," she
said now.

He screamed and bellowed for a while, marching around his
little office above the theater, but finally settled down to predict
sardonically, "There won't be a Saturday performance if you go
on Friday night."

"Word of mouth will fill every seat," said Phyllis. "I've got some good ideas."

Her prediction proved to be on the money. The Friday evening audience comprised six persons, but on Saturday the seats were sold out, in addition to which the SRO crowd was so large as to violate the fire laws, though Kidd got away with only a warning. A bluenosed member of the town council, an elder in his church, tried to close down the production on grounds of obscenity, but he was successfully opposed by two other councilpersons, both eminently respectable wives and mothers, who applauded Phyllis's interpretation of her role as empowering to their sex. A male member pointed out that ticket buyers from elsewhere would bring much-needed revenue to the town, a matter of interest to the several officials who owned local retail businesses.

The review in the weekly newspaper was written by a man named Monroe Calthorp, who not only taught Speech at the high school but had also on a visit to London attended a professional production of Shakespeare in the poet's homeland, though not, admittedly, *Macbeth*. He had roundly derided Kidd's first cast, scorning Jane Wilhelm's performance even more than that of Douglas Bigelow. "One begins to silently scream No, No, No on her first line, having already been put off by her appearance. A hefty Lady Macbeth? I don't think so. What's worse, a Valley Girl's diction."

But Phyllis's conquest of Calthorp was so overwhelming as to give him a different view even of Bigelow, whose stumbling gait and slurred speech he saw as enhancing the emotional disintegration of the character. As to Phyllis, "Never before, at least in this reviewer's ken, has sexuality been used so appropriately, so eloquently at the service of characterization. That Ms. Pierce is comely, that exposing her unclad figure might well run the risk of distracting from the sublime language are serious considerations. The good news is that this does not occur. The power of Shakespeare's words is if anything enhanced by Ms. Pierce, even when she is not the speaker thereof but only stands and waits."

This production of the play was not the first to feature nudity, which had apparently been done a time or two in the hippie era, with Lady Macbeth naked in the sleepwalking scene; and more recently a version of the Three Witches had been offered at a Florida strip club, in a kind of ruse to evade the anti-obscenity laws. But Phyllis was the first on record to incorporate overt sexual acts at moments when they did not pervert, but rather enhanced what William Shakespeare surely intended— and of course in no instance was his celebrated language altered. For example, in Act III, Scene 4, when Banquo's Ghost takes Macbeth's place at the table, Lady Macbeth reproves her husband for his fright:

> Shame itself!
> Why do you make such faces? When all's done,
> You look but on a stool.

And to prove her point, hikes up her gown and gives the Ghost a lap dance, after a few moments of which, its bluff called, the Ghost vanishes as called for in the stage directions.

When, twenty-odd lines later, the apparition reappears, displaying a lustful grin and heading for the lady, the Thane of Cawdor has recovered sufficient self-possession to cry:

Thy bones are marrowless, thy blood is cold;
Thou hast no speculation in those eyes
Which thou dost glare with!

To divert the attention of the others at the table, Scottish noblemen who, not seeing the Ghost, show dismay at Macbeth's bizarre comportment, Phyllis at this point begins to strip while saying:

Think of this, good peers,
But as a thing of custom: 'tis no other,
Only it spoils the pleasure of the time.

As the lords stare at her uncovered breasts, Macbeth sends the Ghost hence and says, "I am a man again."

In the private scenes in their bedroom, the Macbeths conclude their colloquies on criminal ambition with Lady Macbeth. as dominatrix, tying her husband to the bedstead and flogging his bare behind with a cat-o'-nine-tails as the curtain falls. (Unpredictably, Doug Bigelow did not balk at exposing his bum; the whip was made of velvet.)

With a greater attendance for the Saturday performance than any other of his productions had enjoyed for the entire season, Kidd certainly did not close *Macbeth* at the end of its normal run. Rather, he raised ticket prices and next petitioned the school board to permit him to move the play to the capacious auditorium of the public high school. The granting of such permission was delayed only by a dickering over the percentage of the gate that would go to the educational institution. The principal discounted Kidd's argument that the cultural gain to the community should not be assessed in dollars and cents.

Kidd's pleasure in his first real hit was also diminished by the demand of the hitherto unpaid actors to participate in it monetarily. In this they were abetted by Phyllis, who frustrated Kidd's effort to drive a wedge between her and the rest of the cast.

"No, Howard, you and the school board cannot keep the entire income for yourselves. There would be no production without the actors."

"These no-talent amateurs can easily be replaced. The audiences come to see *you*, Phyl. And you're being paid."

"A hundred dollars per week is not very much." As she had been assured by Doug Bigelow. Phyllis still did not quite understand money, and she determined to do research into the subject when she could spare a moment from Shakespearean matters; the Scottish Play, despite Kidd's theory to the contrary, was unlikely to draw crowds forever, according to what she had observed of human fickleness, and she was already planning for its successor, probably *The Merry Wives of Windsor*.

"I'm doubling it on the spot," said Kidd.

"I believe you are an unscrupulous man, Howard," Phyllis told him. "Now that you've increased the performances to six per week, and the ticket price is twenty-five dollars, between seventy-five and a hundred thousand comes into the box office. Unless half this sum is split amongst the actors, I will walk out and stage a rival production at Our Lady of Mercy Academy. I've already got an okay from the Mother Superior."

Kidd was bitter, saying that Catholics would do anything for a buck, but he had no choice except to agree to Phyllis's terms.

The cast members were initially pleased to hear of the new deal Phyllis had negotiated, but their acceptance proved brief. Doug Bigelow believed he should, in the title role, get half the take, whereas the actors who played the other principal parts

maintained that the first dozen names on the traditional drama-
tis personae should get equal amounts, at which the women
protested vigorously, for even the leading female characters,
including Lady Macbeth, were not listed until the roster of
males was exhausted. Those who played the Witches were especially vocal. They were certain, based on fan mail, stage-door
Johnnies, and obscene phone calls (they had previously been
moonlighting from fast-food jobs), that a significant proportion
of the audiences was attracted to the theater by *their* topless performances.

When Phyllis suggested that counting the number of lines
spoken by the respective characters (an easy job for her) and
basing the payments thereupon, several persons, beginning
with old Ned Stilling, who played both Banquo and Banquo's
silent Ghost, made vociferous objection: words were never the
sole medium of the actor's art, else radio drama would still reign
supreme.

The issue was resolved by a deus ex machina. Word of
mouth had quickly made Phyllis's production of *Macbeth* locally
famous. A week or so more was required before the news
reached the city and caught the attention of that drama critic
who was ever alert to new trends and voices, as well as representatives of Actors' Equity, who promptly came out and signed up
the whole cast, thereby taking on the matter of salaries, a favorable development to everybody except Howard Kidd.

But the critic returned to town and wrote a scathingly negative review that dismayed everyone but Phyllis, who predicted
that with such a conspicuous advertisement the production
would acquire national fame, the reviewer having labeled it
as sheer pornography, indeed the most egregious kind that poses
as art.

And she was right, as usual. The area TV channels sent reporters, most of whose stories were picked up by the national networks the next evening, and the print media soon followed. Phyllis was interviewed many times, but her reluctance to provide much personal information frustrated the news weeklies and celebrity mags, for neither could they track her through other sources. She was therefore portrayed as a mysterious personage who had come from nowhere. Added to the allure of this were professional notoriety, physical beauty, and, except as concerned her personal life, a refreshing candor in interviews. (For example, Q: "Are you using sex to sell Shakespeare?" A: "Of course." Q: "Do you feel that cheapens Shakespeare?" A: "Being real, the art of William Shakespeare cannot be cheapened by sex that is simulated." Q: "Do you yourself have a sex life?" A: "I'm not sure I have a life.")

The last response was taken to be modesty, whether actual or phony; columnists differed. Appearing on a TV talk show, the host of which asked questions only to interrupt every answer with a quip or another question as soon as she began to speak, Phyllis said, "My function here is to provide you with straight lines."

"Well," said the host, mugging at the camera, "I'm notoriously straight."

"Then play with yourself," said Phyllis, who unhooked her lapel mike and left the set. This sequence was replayed endlessly on the entertainment-news shows of rival networks.

In short order, and without further effort, Phyllis acquired an agent, a personal manager, a public-relations director, and a contract for the leading female role in a big-budget motion picture.

A fortnight after her departure from the cast, the audiences for *Macbeth* had diminished to the degree that the production was asked to leave the school auditorium. Having returned to the little theater from which it had come, the play closed within the month. When the scales fell from their eyes, its former local promoters agreed with the resuscitated prudes that the show was filth and admitted they had been blinded, though perhaps justifiably, by the superb artistry of Phyllis Pierce.

Meanwhile, Ellery Pierce, her onlie begetter, had fallen into such a state of degradation as to be totally unaware of the success of his creation.

9

Before long Pierce had exhausted his severance payment, and having spent every cent over the years on the development of Phyllis, he had no savings. He was forced to sell his apartment at a low price in a depressed market, and most of the money was claimed by the bank that held the loan. His credit cards were canceled when the respective balances reached their limits.

He exiled himself for a time at his country hideaway, which he owned outright, but he was haunted by memories of Phyllis, whom he had assembled there in the garage workshop. He was almost relieved when a sudden rise in the real-estate taxes forced him to sell that, too, for a song.

Eventually he found himself obliged to make a nightly choice between the streets and a homeless shelter. His clothes were tattered; in daylight his skin was swarthy with dirt but it looked ghostly pale under streetlights after dark. He started to beg. His manner was whinily importunate, but if refused a handout he could turn surly with passersby. After too many such incidents he was picked up by the cops and not arrested but worked over and dropped off in the next precinct, where after some losing encounters with other derelicts jealous of their turf, he finally acquired enough street wisdom not merely to survive but to prosper relative to his fellows in that mean milieu, having learned to disregard rather than compete with them. His early mistake had been to boast about who he used to be, for they all had their own stories, according to which he had fallen amidst ex-generals, former tycoons, and at least one defrocked cardinal.

Ever in need of a female connection, Pierce befriended a runaway teen, who responded to the genteel ways he still had, even down here, with womenfolk. The pair lived in a crawl space under a viaduct and washed, when they could, in public facilities. They were hustled by do-gooders even more than by the police, and eventually the girl, Ali, was persuaded—mostly by Ellery, who degraded though he was had not lost all values— to climb into a van that took her away to a rehabilitation program, and he was alone again.

One thing Ellery could say for himself, even at this stage, was that he never considered suicide. Until now he had nursed a modicum of hope that somehow, in some magical way rather than by volitional effort, things would turn around for him. Now the loss of all hope took with it the ability even to think about doing away with himself. He had barely enough energy to crawl out from under the viaduct and panhandle the price of a wine cooler or search for edibles in the dumpsters outside fast-food restaurants. He would also pick up discarded newspapers, the all-purpose accessory to life on the streets, used for almost anything but reading: clothing-insulator, sole-padder, tinder, ass-wipe.

Ellery rarely spared a glance for the photographs in such

papers, and the textual matters could have been printed in Mandarin for all he cared. Why read of what happened the day before in a world in which he did not participate? As to the pictures, they were of people whose utility for him was nil unless he could harass them in the flesh.

But one day as, in anticipation of an unseasonably chilly night, he lined with newsprint the formerly navy but now green jacket of an ancient suit, he caught sight, by the flicker of a little illegal campfire, of features poignantly familiar in a universe to which he was otherwise all but blind.

It was a picture of Phyllis, his Phyllis! Any doubt that it was the very woman he had constructed from scratch could not be entertained. Display type trumpeted: PHYLLIS IS BACK, MORE BEAUTIFUL, MORE DANGEROUS THAN EVER. It was a full-page advertisement for a movie, depicting her in a two-piece suit of body armor, seemingly of polished brass but brief as the parts of a bikini. On her head was an elaborate helmet that sprouted steel horns or spikes, and her shins were encased in chromium-plated greaves.

Beneath the metallic bra, her breasts in this artist's rendering seemed to have grown several cup sizes from the bosom molded so delicately by Pierce. Brandishing a triumphant sword, she stood with one stiletto-heeled boot on the chest of a fallen warrior, a gargantuan mass of naked muscle in fur habiliments, hairy-faced, grimacing. Phyllis's own countenance was cold and insensate, much less human-looking than when she had been with Ellery. In fact, she looked like a robot, for the first time.

This was a transforming moment for Pierce. His recovery was not instantaneous—he had fallen too far—but at least a corner had been turned.

10

A problem Phyllis sometimes had in her movie career was in finding sufficient private time in which to charge her batteries. Once you become a star, you are seldom alone, especially if you appear in one box-office smash after another. You are surrounded by aides and servitors, cultivated by a range of those who hope to profit by your proximity, adored by multi-tudes, and menaced by more than a few of the deranged. Human performers who enjoy great success often complain of its deleterious effect on one's personal existence. Phyllis did not suffer from such a disadvantage. She did not seek love or to be accepted as an individual with a mind of her own. She was innocent of the urge to voice social concerns or political senti-ments, for she had none to make known. Publicity tours could not exhaust her. She did not use alcohol or drugs, let alone abuse them, and she literally ate nothing, which abstention attracted no notice from a media voracious for the particulars of her private life, for it went without saying that female movie luminaries normally starved themselves.

Throughout the making of her first two pictures, Phyllis was a director's dream, doing exactly what she was told in every scene, but on reading an influential critic's review of the second, she learned that she had been misguided to appear nude in so many shots: "Her body, however shapely, is becoming a cliché." From that point on, she was no longer compliant and soon earned the reputation of being difficult to work with. She questioned the director at every juncture, argued about interpretations, camera angles, lighting, the timing of dialogue, even the competency of her co-stars, who, as of her third film, found their names billed below hers irrespective of their former renown, for Phyllis had no near rival, male or female, in box-office appeal. She would still appear in the nude, but only once during the picture and for a limited time, thus making this scene that which audiences awaited most eagerly. College students were even said to make bets on just when her breasts would be revealed, and also on whether she would show anything below the waist.

Phyllis's early movies were of the action genre. In the first she played a peasant girl during some bygone age of barbarism when her sort served as spoils of war for brutal invaders. But Phyllis's character will not submit to a would-be rapist. She not only resists, she does him in with his own battle-ax. For this deed she is exalted by the oppressed villagers and becomes their leader against the common foe, and her cause prevails. Reviewers generally saw it as a Joan of Arc rip-off, without religion and with sex (she undresses frequently and beds the prince of a neighboring land) and, of course, a happy ending. Moviegoers made it No. 1 in the week of its opening, and it stayed there for a month.

The next picture, derided by the critics as a remake of the

first with only minor dissimilarities (more ambitious special effects: castles with celestial battlements, swords that produced thunder and lightning, nuclear pyrotechnics), were even greater commercial successes. For the third, Phyllis's representatives hammered out a history-making deal: multimillions up front, with a hefty share of the gross. Her face appeared on three national magazine covers, and in the same week she was the sole subject of Cirella Fleming's top-rated celebrity interview. Cirella got a television exclusive and considered it a coup.

CIRELLA: Now, I know this makes you uncomfortable, but our viewers, along with the rest of the *universe* [*leans toward Phyllis, simpering*], are dying to learn a little something about your personal life.

PHYLLIS: It doesn't make me uncomfortable. It's just that I don't have a life beyond my work.

CIRELLA: [*Giggles*] I'm assuming you have a home, a place where, as the man said, when you come there they have to let you in.

PHYLLIS: Yes. I have a home.

CIRELLA: [*Moving in stage-incredulity*] That's *it?*

PHYLLIS: It's a great big house, on—

CIRELLA: Oh, don't say where!

PHYLLIS: There's all kinds of security there.

CIRELLA: I'm sure there is. . . . But I guess what we *really* want to know is not about real estate, but rather about the woman. [*Intensely*] Phyllis, who *are* you?

PHYLLIS: I've had a lot of good fortune.

CIRELLA: [*Still staring fixedly*] You are one tough nut to
crack. But [*smiling radiantly*] we're going to keep
trying—when we come back after this commercial moment.

But Cirella got no more from Phyllis then than before, for there
was no more to be had.

On the advice of her manager, Hal Wintergreen, whose sister was a realtor, Phyllis had indeed purchased a mansion in
Beverly Hills, equipped with a home gym that it would have
been pointless for her to use, and a swimming pool in which she
could not immerse any part of herself lest she short out a circuit.
(Ellery had not gone beyond making her rainproof.)

A half-dozen other persons and two Dobermans were always
on the premises or roaming the grounds; some were servants,
one was a live-in personal assistant, and others worked for the
security service, as did the Dobies, who initially sniffed Phyllis's
feet and subsequently ignored her utterly.

So far Phyllis would go, but when, having got her the house,
Wintergreen urged her to entertain influential figures in the
Industry as well as selected members of the elite media, she
declined.

"I'm where I am only because of the public," said she. "I'll
stay on top, without currying anyone's favor, only if they keep
buying tickets. If they stop, no social connections or favorable
publicity will save my career."

Wintergreen told his intimates and a series of expensive
hookers that he bet Phyllis was the coldest piece of ass anyone
ever tried to shtup, but he had picked up no suggestion that she
was a dyke or swung both ways. Fact was, she had never been
seen with anyone of either sex who could be called a date. "We

got straight, we got gay, we got bi, but she must be some fourth persuasion," he speculated. "A non- or nun."

Phyllis's concern was that after her third action film she was typecast, and the studio executives agreed wholeheartedly, for that's what made the big bucks; exit polls proved that many patrons, especially the youthful, were repeat customers. She was a woman with whom girls, straight or Lesbian, could identify, but as it turned out, also one whom heterosexual young men would most like to be beaten up by (in fantasy), and gays thought of her as a protector (in her second movie, Phyllis makes short work of a crude warrior who bullies a zither-strumming bard).

"Be that as it may," said she, "I am a unique commodity. No one else has had my kind of success with such pictures, though they've certainly tried. The difference obviously is *me*. I am one of a kind. The public will come to see me in any kind of story. Females love to see me win. Males all want to fuck me." Ordinarily Phyllis avoided the use of foul language, but this was the sort of people with whom it was advisable to talk turkey, as they listened in their designer suits and three-hundred-dollar haircuts.

"They'll all come to see me in serious drama—did I not start out with Shakespeare?—and in love stories, too! And you know what I'm looking forward to most? A classic screwball comedy, with sparkling dialogue and absurd situations involving animals and goofy sidekicks, mistaken identities, the whole shmeer. The girl and the guy kick it off by hating each other on sight—they get trapped in the country in a storm and have to take cover in a stable. . . . I might even write the script!"

Afterward, in her absence, the suits agreed that Phyllis herself had become the classic cunt all female superstars are by their third box-office smash, whereas a male turns prick after just the first, but then, come on, he's a guy. They would dread dealing with her from now on, but if she played hardball they really had no option except to submit, at least once.

As good as her word, Phyllis wrote a screenplay and further-more did so in a matter of days, entitling it, literally, *Screwball Comedy*. A female studio executive with a taste for the classic genre recognized it immediately as a blatant plagiarism, with scene after scene lifted from the 1930s–40s pictures of Capra, Hawks, Sturges, and others, and with a female lead for Phyllis that amalgamated roles played originally by the likes of Claudette Colbert, Katharine Hepburn, and Irene Dunne.

The executive asked the ironic question, "But where's your Cary Grant?"

Literal as always, Phyllis said, "We'll have to look hard, no doubt about it."

"Phyllis, your sources are awfully obvious."

"I chose the best of the best."

"I don't think we can get away with that."

Phyllis pointed out that remakes were being done all the time.

"That's not quite the same thing."

"I don't see why not," Phyllis said. "I've brought the presen-tation up to date."

"You mean, with the sex."

"Exactly."

"When the walls of Jericho fall, Clark and Claudette are shown doing the nasty. When the back of Hepburn's dress is torn away, we see, instead of lace underpants, your bare ass."

"But most of the nudity occurs when they are stranded on the island."

"Irene Dunne and Randolph Scott, *My Favorite Wife*, right?

With all respect, I don't think it will fly, Phyllis." And the male executives all agreed. But Phyllis strong-armed them into making the film, to everyone's dismay—including even that of the director who was her handpicked rubber stamp.

The Cary Grant substitute, who was Phyllis's choice to play her love interest, came from one of the soap operas she canvassed, taping them to view during the wee hours, for since she had become famous she could not roam her old all-night haunts. Only Phyllis believed Wayne Upshaw had more than superficial talent, and all others were appalled when they watched the dailies and saw the youngster's awkward attempts to simulate Grant's signature moves and unique Bristol-cum-California accent. But Phyllis was vociferously pleased with his performance, and to the universal objections replied, consistently plagiaristic, "The kid stays in the picture."

Preview audiences throughout Orange County went wild, inscribing their cards, "The funniest ever!" "Pants-wetting comedy!" "I'm going to keep laughing all week." "Who knew somebody so beautiful and sexy could be side-splittingly comical? Who knew?" Upshaw, too, got kudos. "The hunky Englishman is a find!" "Wayne is a dream!" "Sophisticated but cute."

When *Screwball Comedy* opened to the general public, however, the reviews were mixed. Some of the critics thought it pathetic; the remainder, outrageous. The latter took it as a satire so heavy-handed as to be simply insulting to the beloved genre. The others thought the picture was sincerely made by naïve, inept practitioners who were beyond their depth when trying to make the transition from shallow action flicks to the subtleties of social comedy.

But the box-office figures went through the roof, and the

beauty was that the film cost so little to make, with the exception of Phyllis's large fee plus her cut of the gross. Upshaw, however, and a supporting cast of unknowns were paid peanuts.

Notwithstanding Phyllis's resounding success, earned against the will of the studio executives, the same gentry was opposed to her next project, which would be still another departure. She wanted to do *Camille*, the tragic story of the courtesan who dies of consumption and for love, previously brought to the screen many times, most notably by Greta Garbo, but quite another thing than Phyllis had demonstrated a talent for. True, she had gotten away with what was really farce, but tragedy was a much further cry. Could she pass for tubercular, whatever the magic of makeup? Could she show the depth of feeling that the role called for? Throughout the action pictures and the comedy as well, she had been restrained as to emotional display, but the character of Camille cried out for an intensity without extravagance, the kind of thing that had been Garbo's great strength, to which her ethereal face and marked but soft accent contributed so profoundly. Phyllis was so *American* for a role that was European to the hilt, unless she was thinking of changing its fictional milieu to the contemporary United States, which would hardly fly. Nobody died for love nowadays.

"I intend to go back to the novel written by Alexandre Dumas *fils*," said Phyllis, "and follow the text to the letter, beginning with the real title, *The Lady of the Camellias*, and the heroine's name is Marguerite Gauthier."

Having learned French in her spare time, Phyllis had read *La Dame aux camélias*, and she was a stickler for authenticity.

There was even worse news: This was to be the first of Phyllis's pictures without any nudity whatsoever, and in fact, with no sex scenes.

"Jesus!" cried one of the executives. "Camille's supposed to be a courtesan, isn't she? No sex in a movie about a whore?"

"That's the point," Phyllis explained. "We play against type. We'll give 'em what they don't expect. I started that with my little-theater Scottish Play, which is why I am here today. I know how the taste of the public works. Look at my box-office figures."

That was always the clincher: what made money must prevail, else things would go out of order.

The Lady of the Camellias was Phyllis's first success with the critics, to the degree that several of the influential ones began to revise their negative assessments of her earlier work, seeing it now as a series of campy send-ups, done over the top so as to make a joke of the joke. *The Lady* was simply too good, too sensitive, too finely conceived and crafted to have been preceded by infantile action pictures and a humorless comedy. Something deeper must have been in play all along.

More than one reviewer, familiar with the 1937 *Camille* from film-festival screenings or videotape, saw a credible *hommage* to Garbo in Phyllis's performance. Some even found Phyllis's face to have acquired a Garbo-like luminescence, an internal glow beyond the art of the most ingenious director of lighting. Her voice also found special praise. It was lower-pitched than before and, though Phyllis spoke Standard American, employed slight hesitation here and there that seemed to hover on the brink of an unspecified accent. And she was universally praised for having gone beyond the cruder forms of sexual display.

The critics' first was soon followed by one on the part of the public. For the first time ever, audiences hated a movie starring Phyllis Pierce. People walked out during the picture, in theaters from coast to coast. Billboards advertising the film were defaced, often obscenely. The movie and its star were derided nightly on the TV comedy shows. After two weeks of this, the distributors pulled *The Lady* from screens all over the country, though they waited awhile overseas, where it was not doing all that badly even if falling far behind Phyllis's previous pictures (except, perhaps because of cultural chauvinism, in France, for of all the versions done by foreigners, including Giuseppe Verdi's *La Traviata*, this was the most faithful to the original; and Phyllis herself had, with a *bon accent*, dubbed the soundtrack). Still, the foreign grosses could not save the movie from being a big-time bomb.

When the dust had settled, Phyllis readily admitted she had been wrong (which the people who account for such matters said was yet another difference between her and any other star of her magnitude) and agreed that the best move would be hastily to shoot another of her surefire action pictures. This was quickly done, with the old nudity back and then some—severe cuts had to be made to claim its "R"—but the public, once betrayed, did not return, seemingly agreeing at last with the critics, who returned to shit-jobbing Phyllis but with a new venom. She was said to have lost the few virtues she had displayed as an action star. Her old spark was gone, she was showing her age, she had put on weight. All of which was literally impossible so long as her batteries were charged, and she considered revealing her nonhumanity to expose the lies for what they were, but decided against doing so because revealing she was not of flesh and blood might lead to a discrediting of her work in general. By now she knew something about human responses, which, defying reason, were usually evoked rather by fancy than fact, by what is *preferred* rather than what *is*.

It was at this point, the lowest in possibilities since Phyllis's career began, that Ellery Pierce came back into what, for lack of a more precise term, must be called her life.

11

The newspaper display seen by the derelict Pierce had been an advertisement for *Fur and Steel*, which was intended to be Phyllis's comeback film after the box-office disaster. Until that moment he had been altogether ignorant of any part of her existence after she left him, and he knew nothing of the highs and lows of her years in show business. When he panhandled enough money for a ticket to see *Fur and Steel*, he sat in awe. She was magnificent! What had he wrought?

But he had to admit that Phyllis had gone far beyond that with which he had supplied her. For one, she had somehow grown more beautiful, and it was more than makeup. Her voice was richer than the capabilities of his original sound system would allow. Had she since been altered by a superior technician? Though, after much effort, he had developed for her a stride that was regular enough to meet human standards, with arm and body movements that were inconspicuously normal, Phyllis would never have been taken for an athlete. Now here she was, whirling, leaping, wielding two swords windmill-style, simultaneously; somersaulting in thin air, backflipping from heights, all with extraordinary ease, even grace, and it was *she*, in shot after shot, and not a stuntwoman—Pierce looked at movies with the eye of a pro. There were few camera tricks in Phyllis's scenes and little computer enhancement. How had she learned to do these things and from whom? She was persistently exceeding her capacity.

Phyllis as she existed today was inexplicable to him. She represented an impossibility. Her handlers must know, by now, that she was an artificial woman. They *had* to know. They had updated or replaced her major systems and reprogrammed her completely. She was no longer the Phyllis that Pierce had created and, in retrospect, loved so profoundly. Given the nature of her being, it could not even be said that she had grown, human-style, from what she once had been to what she was today, as a girl becomes a woman. She had rather evolved, like successive models of an automobile, from Model T to Lincoln Town Car, or like the telephone, from Bell's crude experiment to today's miniature portable instrument. She had not matured; she had undergone a series of modifications.

Phyllis was no longer a feasible substitute for a real woman. She had become, in the truest sense of a word that has no necessary moral connotation, a monster.

Nevertheless Pierce was more intrigued with her than ever. His aim now was to reestablish contact at any cost. He realized the risks inherent in this endeavor. It was likely that the creature he had built from scratch would not even recognize him. And were that to happen, he would be devastated. Yet he approached that possibility, perhaps even likelihood, not as a moth to the flame (moths do so through naïvety, not a taste for immolation) but as a man besotted by love.

12

Phyllis could have been as good at finance as she was at everything else, but while she had been distracted by creative pursuits her business manager embezzled an amount of money that would take a while to calculate exactly but was in the millions and constituted most of what she owned aside from her mansion, which she was forced to sell at a loss, paying the proceeds to creditors.

As it turned out, her other employees had incurred large expenses in her name, and she, whose personal tastes were frugal, had to pay for vintage beverages and luxurious provender consumed by her staff, their upscale transportation, and even the clothes and jewelry they wore.

The pictures she was offered now were of the straight-to-cable type and paid what her current manager (the previous one had jumped ship when he detected shoals ahead) called "short money," by accepting which she would set foot on a descent from which, given the law of career inertia, few had ever returned. His advice was to seek second-female lead parts in big-budget films, say best friend to the star, or even character roles now that she was maturing.

Phyllis of course had not aged a month since her first picture, nor would she get older in a human sense if she lived forever. She might become outmoded by new technological developments, though she had not as yet seen evidence of any such. So far as she knew, she was the only animatronic actor to have come so far. It was possible that others had tried, but unlike members of some ethnic groups, they did not make common cause. Assemblages of plastic and metal tend not to identify with one another.

After disposing of her mansion, Phyllis moved into an apartment hotel where a number of formerly noted performers lived who were in forced semiretirement. Some were in rehabilitation from an indulgence in harmful substances inhaled, ingested, or injected. Others, like Phyllis, had either gone beyond or fallen behind the tastes of their original audiences and had not as yet been able to acquire replacements. Hasbrook House was unfortunately named for its 1940s builder, a nonentertainer who could not have foreseen that it would inevitably come to be known (by its residents; nobody else cared) as Hasbeen House; excepting the rare ex-addict who had actually cleaned up his or her act, the place was a refuge for negative thinkers behind masks of pseudo-optimism.

Incapable of discouragement, Phyllis kept her own counsel and went her own way. She starred in a few obscure movies, shown only in the wee hours on major urban television markets, and eventually took the role as madam of a luxury call-girl service in a continuing cable series. One thing she would never stoop to, however, was a subordinate part in any production in which there was a more prominent female of greater intended sexual attraction. She would never allow herself to be typecast as a runner-up, a second banana.

It was at Hasbeen House that Ellery finally caught up with her after many months of searching. He lacked the sources of old, had too long been away from his show-business past, and in any event would have been embarrassed to try to reconnect in his current situation. But he was no longer in the ranks of society's castoffs, and now made an honest living as a humble handyman, applying his technical abilities to the likes of replacing a trap under a washbasin or the ball float in a toilet tank, servicing air-conditioner compressors, and various sorts of electrical rewiring.

Phyllis had no need for plumbing or heating and cooling—people who worked with her on films sometimes noticed she did not sweat even when under the sun on desert locations—but she did require light for reading and using the computer, and when one day the power went off in her apartment, she intercommed the Hasbeen's basement maintenance man.

When he appeared she recognized him immediately though the light was poor on an overcast day.

"Ellery, is the electricity off just here or throughout the entire building?"

"God Almighty, *Phyllis!*" For a few instants Pierce was too overwhelmed to speak coherently. Under the assumption he was choking, Phyllis thumped him between the shoulder blades, but, not aware of her own strength, almost knocked him down.

He ducked and stepped aside, gaining the strength to cry, "I've found you at last!"

"I haven't been lost, Ellery. It is true that my career is not what it once was, but you can't stay on top forever. Maybe some do, but someone like me cannot ignore the law of averages."

"Phyllis, may I touch you?"

"Must you ask? You constructed me, Ellery."

He put his arms around her. She was the very same Phyllis he had built years before, as soft and warm, firm but yielding, velvet skin and silken hair. "I've always been crazy about you, Phyl. Did you miss me?"

"Ellery, I am incapable of that kind of feeling."

It had been a stupid question, and he apologized for asking it.

"The apology is no less pointless, Ellery, since it can have no effect on me."

"I understand, Phyllis. But *I'm* human and need to be indulged. I realized it could mean nothing to you, but as it happens I'm in love with you."

"Do you want to go to bed?" She was naked under the mauve dressing gown. She usually went about the apartment in the nude, clothes having for her only a social function; she donned some only if answering the door. Recently she had leaned over to point to an out-of-order electrical outlet for Pierce's predecessor, and her breasts, visible through the gaping bosom of the robe, provoked his lust. In subduing the man, Phyllis had broken his jaw, hence the leave of absence that had resulted in Ellery's reappearance.

Pierce was disappointed now, despite himself. "Come on, Phyl. I'm trying to tell you that you were never a mere sex object to me."

"Isn't that why you built me?"

"I don't know. It may have been. If so, I have changed."

"Why?"

"Can we sit down?"

"Of course, Ellery. Anyplace at all."

He chose a sofa and patted the cushion alongside him. "Sit here, Phyllis. . . . I fell on bad times after you left. I hadn't realized your leaving would have such an effect on me—how much I needed you, how much I loved you. I know, it's irrational to have such feelings. I'm aware that right now I could open that panel concealed under the hair on your crown and disconnect you. I *know* that, but I don't really believe it."

"You're delusional, Ellery, but probably no more so than all human beings are about one thing or another. Your irrationality is why you build machines, the function of which is to be unfailingly rational and compensate for your weakness."

"I can take credit for making you beautiful, but what I don't understand is how you can be more intelligent than I programmed you to be."

"Obviously, that's something I cannot explain," said Phyllis. "As a human being cannot smell its own breath. But if the matter distresses you, you might forget it for a while anyway by fucking me."

A shocked Pierce chided her. "I never taught you to talk like that."

"I picked that up in show business, a foul-mouthed venue, Ellery. I won't say it again."

"You cannot be apologized to," he observed wonderingly. "Yet you can apologize."

"That makes sense, Ellery. Think about it. *You* made *me*, not vice versa."

"Do you suppose, Phyllis, that since you have this extraordinary capacity for developing unlikely powers, that some time you might be able to love me?"

"I could do it right now, Ellery. Just tell me to."

"That can't be done with love. It must be freely offered."

He could not remember having provided Phyllis with a means for displaying puzzlement, but he must have done so, for a vertical line appeared between her knitted eyebrows. "That's a new one on me."

Pierce took her immaculate hand, which was of normal warmth. "Your original heating system seems to be still working."

"Everything you built functions as well as when I was brand new," Phyllis said. "You are a master craftsman, Ellery."

He looked deep into her limpid hazel eyes, in which he would defy anyone to find the slightest suggestion she was not real. "I've never been able to build another woman, Phyllis. I broke the mold after producing you."

"In a mold?"

"Just an expression," said he. "Meaning you are absolutely unique."

"That statement is tautological, Ellery. 'Unique' is already an absolute, like 'perfect.'"

"Or 'pregnant,'" Pierce said. "How would you feel about becoming a mother, Phyl?"

"I wouldn't feel any—"

"Let me rephrase that. Suppose I build us a baby. Could you be a mother?"

"Sure," Phyllis said in her affectionate manner, even returning his soft squeeze of the hand. "As it will never change, you must be prepared to produce a series of animatronic children, each at another stage of life."

Now it was Pierce who frowned. "You're right. I don't know whether I can rise to that challenge."

"Oh," Phyllis said, patting his hand. "Of course we can,

Ellery. 'But screw your courage to the sticking-place / And we'll not fail.'"

"Where'd that come from?"

"The Scottish Play, by William Shakespeare."

He put his arm around her, kissed her left ear, and spoke into her hair at the temple. "Have you been faithful to me? Don't answer that."

Phyllis stirred in his arms. "Ellery, the electricity is still off. See the clock on the mantelpiece?"

"I'll look into that matter in a minute."

"Would you like me to make you a gimlet and cook a meal of potage Germiny, veal Orloff, fonds d'artichaut, baby carrots—"

"We'd miss a great opportunity if you went back to being a housewife, Phyl. Your show-biz career may have taken a downturn, but you are still a celebrity to millions of people." He loosened his embrace to lean away and look into her perfect face. "I'm thinking about politics, Phyllis. Tell me you can't go all the way to the Presidency."

"I can't do it."

"What?"

"You just told me to tell you that."

"I was speaking rhetorically. You can do it."

"Naturally," said Phyllis. She frowned again. "Ellery, you'd better tell me what the Presidency is. I have accumulated an amount of knowledge, but there are still gaps in it, I'm sure."

Pierce got to his feet and pulled her up to join him. He reached inside the dressing gown, slipping his arms around her slender waist, interlocking his fingers at the smooth groove in the small of her back, which he himself had sculptured. "You're a quick study. Meanwhile, let's do go to bed." He was out of practice at sex and could not guarantee a satisfactory performance. But what would Phyllis care? . . . On the other hand, was that good? Should he rather program her to demand that he follow her lead in always rising above minimal expectations? Can even the artificially feminine draw us ever upward?

"Sex is one thing, Ellery," said Phyllis, "but I'll have to be convinced that giving you an influential role in my career makes sense. After all, I went to the top without any help from you."

"It wasn't because I denied it to you, if you remember," he pointed out. "It's even possible that you would have stayed up there had I been around. . . . I'm no longer just a technician, Phyl. I've learned a lot about life outside the lab. Hitting the bottom is an educational experience. You can call that trite, but it's true."

"I believe you are speaking tautologically, Ellery," said she.

13

On reuniting with Phyllis, Pierce began still another phase of his life, in its early stage the most difficult of all to accept. In a way, hitting bottom had been easier, because at least some form of self-determination had been in effect there, whereas now, uniquely in his experience, he was professionally inferior to the person with whom he was most intimate. Phyllis was the one with the career, which he could not compromise by remaining in the employment of Hasbeen House, though she herself, perhaps because she did not have a proper self, did not understand until he explained.

"I'm pleased you haven't become a snob," said he. "But most human beings cannot afford to be otherwise, the natural competitive urge being what it is."

"To compete, must one despise competitors?"

"No, Phyllis. Competitors are to be respected."

"Ellery, I want you to know that I have nothing against human beings. I realize that I was created by one."

He wondered whether she meant this ironically, which

would be evidence of still another level of character development, but decided, looking into her guileless eyes, that she was
being literal as always.

"That's reassuring. If you can't love me, at least you don't
think of me as an enemy."

"That would be foolish. You did not build me to be a fool but
rather to be proficient at whatever I undertake."

The statement did not accurately represent his original aim,
but he could not at the outset have foreseen the extraordinary
result.

"We should seriously review our prospects," said he. "I have
no money whatever, and not having practiced my profession for
some years, I am at a disadvantage in trying to resume it. I
should have to begin all over again, on the bottom level. That
would be dispiriting at my age."

"Ellery, has it occurred to you that if you revealed to the
world that you designed and constructed me, you would be celebrated everywhere and rewarded handsomely?"

"Just a moment, Phyl. Is that an original idea of your own? I
haven't suggested it in any way, have I?"

"Certainly not. It's entirely mine."

"It would be completely different if I had programmed you to
make that point. It would be no more than self-flattery."

"I understand least when you speak of your *self*. I know I
don't have one, but if I did, it would be yours, would it not?"

The subject was too disturbing for Pierce to explore further
at the time, so he exited from it by asking, "Who does?" Then
quickly added, "That's not a real question."

"Ellery, you've done that frequently of late: asked an apparent question that was really not one."

"I'm thinking out loud, Phyl. It's a great relief to have you nearby again. If I talked to myself when living alone, I worried about my mental balance. . . . Now, as to revealing publicly that you are animatronic, picking the proper moment is essential. We must get maximum exposure, in circumstances as favorable as possible. That is to say, we don't, above all, want the tabloids to get hold of the information first, because if that happens you'll be branded permanently as a freak and you'll never be able to work again except at an amusement park."

"That's still show business, isn't it?"

"A branch, maybe, but it would be unacceptable after your movie career, even though that lately has declined from what it was once. . . . You know, Phyl, if we could just come up with an idea of how to put your career on the up-track again. . . . Something exciting in a positive way. Not a scandal, nothing unsavory. Preferably, you should be seen as lovable. Which of course you already are to me, but that's *me*."

"I haven't been able to get anywhere with my ideas for movies since the box-office fiasco with *The Lady of the Camellias*," Phyllis pointed out. "The public doesn't give a flying fuck for art. Forgive me, Ellery. I am quoting an industry executive."

"I'll tell you this, in my own period of decline I learned to think outside the box, and it wasn't easy. I had been in technology all my life. I was forced to come up with alternatives. I can't say I did well. I sank into degradation, but I survived. In your case shame doesn't enter the picture. You can't be blamed, but you *can* be applauded. Do you get the distinction? If you try something and fail, you're only nonhuman. If you succeed, it's remarkable because you're just a robot."

"Are those called truisms, Ellery?"

"Well said, Phyllis. But I'm getting to the point. You've reached pretty much a dead end as a movie star, and the things

you've been doing lately are insuring that you'll stay there forever: those low-budget straight-to-TV features with that karate
moron who beats up whole street gangs single-handedly, single-
footedly. I saw one the other night at twelve-thirty A.M."

"Off-camera he's a big wuss," Phyllis said. "He kept getting
hurt when we sparred, so stuntmen usually did his fights. They
too sometimes got banged up. It isn't that I don't know my own
strength; it's that I overestimate that of muscular young men in
the best condition."

"What we need, Phyl, is a gimmick. We've got to plan, not
just continue in this haphazard fashion. Time is going by, at
least for me. I've got to get back on top before I'm too old to
make the most of it."

"Of course, Ellery," Phyllis said, and lifted and spread her
thighs.

"I don't mean sex," said he, lying alongside her in bed. "That
was another figure of speech, referring to worldly success. By the
way, Phyl, I haven't forgotten how great you are at making
love."

"And anytime I'm not, you can simply readjust me."

He turned on the pillow, his head so close to hers that had
she been human his face would have been warmed by her
breath. "It's really hard to believe you don't feel anything."

"I could tell you I do if you want."

"No," said Pierce, rising on one elbow and looking ahead.
"It's essential that I never lie to myself. The only way I can keep
this going is not to take it literally."

"That was Macbeth's mistake," Phyllis said. "He should
never have believed those witches. That was all imaginary."

Pierce felt it necessary to point out that the whole play was
fiction.

"But William Shakespeare was a real person, Ellery. That should be taken into consideration."

It was a healthy state of affairs when he got such a reminder that Phyllis had her limitations.

"The gimmick, Phyl, the device by which we can head back up; I'm convinced there is one. We can reveal you're animatronic only when we are in a position of strength. If we do it prematurely it will only keep us where we are."

"If you say so, Ellery."

14

I've given this a lot of thought, Phyllis, and I'm convinced we are on the right track."

"We need an income, Ellery," she pointed out. "Our expenditures far exceed our income, which in fact is almost nil, and our assets have now dwindled to the vanishing point. Don't you think I should accept one of the offers I'm getting?"

They were living in a bungalow in the garden of a luxury hotel, and Pierce had acquired for Phyllis a costly wardrobe from the top designers, as well as an array of the kind of jewelry worn by conspicuous female celebrities, some of which was on loan on the condition that it be displayed at award ceremonies and the lavish parties that followed.

"Absolutely not," he said now. "We take no more short money, nothing but top billing in big-budget productions."

"Thus far nothing of that sort has appeared. Are you sure it will? You are not a personal manager by profession, Ellery. I believe that is quite another thing from the electronic technology of which you are a master."

"My point exactly, Phyl. How hard can it be?" On the basis of his success with Phyllis, Pierce had convinced himself he could do anything to which he applied his will. "We just have to keep up our nerve for a while longer."

"I don't get nervous," Phyllis noted. "I'm just pointing out that our coffers sound / With hollow poverty and emptiness."

"*Macbeth?*"

"*Henry the Fourth, Part Two*, Act One, Scene Three, line seventy-four."

"I haven't been able to attract much interest in bringing your take on *Macbeth* to the screen," Pierce said. "Those who go for the sex don't like the poetry, and vice versa. . . . Maybe you could get involved in some kind of scandal which would result in a legal trial that got national media attention."

"Would you like me to research examples of that?"

"It can't be something that's bad enough to compromise you, like a crime of violence. Maybe repeated incidences of shoplifting? No, that's undignified. The sexual area would seem fruitful, but what and how? Arrested as a street hooker, while posing as one, researching a movie role?"

"How about actually working as a high-priced call girl?" Phyllis asked. "I understand there's a lot of money in that. As a successful whore I wouldn't have to look for movie work."

Pierce snorted. "Thanks for reminding me you're not human. I needed that. Prostitution is commonly regarded as degrading to women, but how could a machine lose the esteem of humanity by anything it did?"

"It's settled then? I'll be a prostitute? A website is the best way to look for customers nowadays, not on a street corner, where not only might the police interfere, but there's the matter of pimps."

"Sorry, Phyl, there I go again, being ironic. I certainly do not intend to prostitute you. I know you don't have any principles, but I do, strange as that might seem in a man who can love only a woman who is artificial. But that doesn't mean I've lost all sense of proportion. Feeling for you what I do, how could I sell you to other men?"

"Is prostitution selling? Isn't it rather renting?"

"Technically true," Pierce admitted. "But there's an entire other dimension in human affairs, one that you are not equipped to understand. A man commonly desires many different women, but would like each of them to desire only himself."

"But Othello cares only for Desdemona. That could be said to be his downfall. Had he an alternative, he might not have killed her, and he certainly would not have committed suicide. For that matter, in the Scottish Play, Macbeth's only female alternatives to his wife are the Witches, and they agree with her in encouraging him in the ambition that destroys him. It might make more sense for a man to have more than one woman at a time, so as to be able to make choices at various junctures."

Pierce peered narrowly at her. "Now, here's an odd situation, Phyl. I made you originally to be the perfect woman for my own taste, but you have gone far beyond my design. Yet I still think you are perfect, and I want no one else. So I am not like the typical man, whom you are apparently urging me to be."

"The fact remains that we need money, Ellery, and I could make some so easily. There must be many rich men who would pay dearly to make the beast with two backs with a movie star."

"Not on your life, Phyllis! Apart from the considerations that have to do with, I grant you, my ego, not to mention the values of an orderly society, such a thing would jeopardize the plans I have for you, once we can find an adequate springboard. Shameful behavior comes back to haunt the participant therein, often years later." He thought for a moment; he was not illiterate. "As Shakespeare said, 'Caesar's wife should be above suspicion.'"

"That line is not to be found in any of Shakespeare's published writings."

"Well, I'm not going to sell your sexual services, period. . . . Wait a minute, I'm getting an idea. Once you study a subject, you acquire an encyclopedic command of it. What about a television quiz show, called something like *Can You Stump Phyllis?* You would be pitted against a panel of recognized experts in various fields. Obviously Shakespeare and old movies, but given a week's notice you could handle any area of human knowledge, am I right?"

"Of course, though it probably wouldn't take as long as a week. It would depend on the availability of recorded research materials, in written language or mathematical symbols."

"I doubt that nuclear physics would have much appeal to a popular audience," Pierce said, "but natural science, especially animals, would attract people, and anything to do with crime, sex, Hitler—"

"What is Hitler?"

"The epitome of evil."

"What is evil?"

"Not the kind of thing," Pierce said, "that you are equipped to comprehend, Phyllis, because there is no universal standard by which it can be assessed. It's a human invention, but human beings have always debated about its definition and generally feel that it's the other fellow's problem. But most of the human race would agree on Hitler. Another widespread conviction is that animals cannot be evil, not even cobras and sharks."

"Why?"

"They're not human."

"Is the same true of animatronic personages?"

"That's right, Phyl, *you* cannot be immoral. If you do something that people consider evil, the blame would be mine."

While Pierce deliberated on the new project, Phyllis surfed the internet to see what information was available. She returned to say, "Ellery, on Google there are one million, seven hundred fifty thousand websites pertaining to Hitler. Shall I go through them?"

"Hold off until I develop this idea further. Your storage capacity isn't infinite, you know. Let's leave room for what we might need in the future."

But Pierce was not able to get far with the project. The TV programmers with whom he talked all more or less agreed that, for this era anyway, quiz programs, whatever their gimmick, had run their course. Reality programming was the trend: a conditionally candid camera followed real people through the events of their everyday lives. Phyllis took this to be a video version of the voyeur porn websites.

"But Ellery," said she, "I don't go to the toilet, and not being altogether waterproof, I can't take a bath or shower. And knowing you, I doubt you would want us to be seen having sex."

"It would be stuff like shopping, eating, talking with friends, going to clubs, none of which you actually ever do, of course."

"But I am an actress," Phyllis said. "It would be playing a

part, like any other. After all, everything I've ever done has been acting. It's necessarily all I *can* do."

"We may have something here," said Pierce. "Your status right now is perfect for reality TV: You're a has-been but still recognizable to much of the public."

15

H *anging Out with Phyllis* was not a success on cable. The
public and the critics were unanimous: As herself Phyllis proved boring. She was not grotesque either in appearance or
manner, and her professed tastes and opinions were reasonable,
as was her language. Pierce in fact now found himself obliged to
urge her to use the occasional bleepable obscenity, to juice up
her dialogue with the actors who played the trio of sidekicks:
the ebony-torsoed former wrestler who served as her personal
trainer; her cook, an effervescent Asian; and her "best friend," a
white female interior designer with a wit that great effort was
expended in the scripting thereof to make acerbic.

This cast of characters had been established after much
research into what audiences might like but also what no significant segment of it would be offended by. Thus the Asian was
not identified specifically as to culture: His eyelids had the epi-
canthic fold, but he could have hailed from anywhere in the
eastern Orient, and he had no discernible accent. The ex-
wrestler, a bulky six-foot-five African Native American (his

maternal grandmother was a Chickasaw), had an Ivy League honors degree and regularly quoted from Keats. Gwen, the best friend, was a professionally successful single mother, who easily found time to juggle a demanding job with the responsibilities of parenthood, yet seemed always to be in Phyllis's company, cracking wise about the decor of the restaurants at which they dined ("taste-deprived") or reflecting waspishly on fictional friends they had in common (botched cosmetic surgery, adulteries, stinginess).

Phyllis privately observed to Pierce that in her opinion Gwen's character provided only a reminder of how inferior it was to the female sidekick of the 1940s films, played classically by Eve Arden, and he did not disagree but pointed out that the kind of people who were today's target audience would not be equipped, or inclined, to make the comparison. And in fact Gwen proved to be the most popular character in the show, more so than Phyllis herself.

According to the surveys taken frequently throughout the early months of the program, Phyllis was the least liked of the four. Young women viewers found her too passive, especially disappointing in an actress who had been celebrated for kicking male ass in the movie roles for which she became famous. Whereas middle-aged women interpreted her reserve as snobbery.

When, in response to Pierce's suggestion that she use saltier language, Phyllis on occasion cried, "Oh sh—!" or "F— that!," first hundreds, then more than a thousand viewers protested by telephone, fax, e- and snail-mail, and the show was attacked publicly by clerical and lay bluenoses. Nor was support forthcoming from advocates of laissez-faire airwaves, for Phyllis took no vocal position on any progressive cause—abortion, gun control, the environment, or the like—and in fact Gwen more than once rolled her eyes and moued when referring to a male interior decorator whose tastes were, "Gawd, over the top!"

The Asian chef Lu's generic stir fries had little appeal, being too exotic for provincial viewers, who could not find the ingredients, and too banal for those in big metropolitan areas where koba noodles, five-spice powder, and garam masala were long passé, and meatloaf, mac'n'cheese, and 'smores were in vogue. As for Ned, the literate giant, he was seen as being either gay, an Uncle Tom, or both, and in any case pompously phony.

The time came when Pierce was obliged to report, "Phyllis, I'm afraid we're being cancelled."

"What's your next idea, Ellery?"

"There's one of your many advantages over me. This is hitting me hard, given the high hopes I had. I really thought we had a winner, didn't you?"

"In fact I did not."

"Then why didn't you say anything?"

"I saw how enthusiastic you were at the outset," Phyllis replied. "Then, what do I know?"

He took her warm face between his hands. After all these years her heating system still functioned perfectly. "Phyl," he said, "you didn't want to hurt my feelings. Are you really beginning to care for me?"

"This is not the first time you've asked me that question or some variation on it, Ellery. Why is it so important? The answer cannot change what I am, or for that matter, what you are."

Unlike human beings, machines knew their own minds. Or did they? In any event, they were immune to either hope or disappointment.

"I'm going to let *you* come up with the next idea," he told her. "You did pretty well on your own."

"All in all, just so-so, Ellery. I got to the top but could not manage to stay there."

"Not many have been able to do that, and so far as I know, no other animatron."

"That's no excuse," Phyllis stated. "I made a thorough study of American movies in their golden era and proceeded accordingly. Greta Garbo left the Industry of her own volition, not because audiences turned against her."

"I just don't know if Garbo was the right model for you, Phyl."

She looked keenly at him, immaculate eyebrows knitting, as he had designed them to do. "I am devoid of any musicality, as you well know. I have no sense of rhythm and can't carry a tune. Nor, though I can run well enough and leap, can I dance for the life of me, else I might have used Betty Grable or Rita Hayworth as models."

"I'll tell you, Phyllis," Pierce said soberly, "I really don't have the nerve to try to retool you at this late date. After my ups and downs, I lack the old confidence. What if I messed up and disabled you in some fashion? I'd never forgive myself. I think we'd better forget musical comedy as a vehicle."

"What's left to try?"

"How about a talk show? I know, there have been all kinds, at all hours of the day, with every type of host, from daytime sobsisters through evening loudmouths to late-night clowns, but you would be the only one ever to know at least as much about the subject in question as the guest, whoever the latter might be."

"Could you explain, Ellery? I have watched a lot of television, but have focused on the informational shows on the Learning, Discovery, and History channels, and of course those that show old movies."

"Basically, guests are interviewed about their current projects. During the day, these are predominantly folks with personal problems, who are brought together with experts who can pretend to solve such. Political types predominate in the evening, and show-biz celebrities on late night. Given your lack of a sense of humor, I think we can rule out the last-named, where interviews with entertainment personalities alternate with comedy routines."

"As you well know, I can laugh," said Phyllis. "But I don't do so unless told to. I can also understand why human beings laugh. In my observation, it's when they perceive that a situation is incomplete but not totally incapable of being completed. Were the latter the case, sadness would be the ruling emotion."

"I have to think about that," said Pierce. "You come up with challenging concepts, Phyl. They would be ideal for a prime-time evening program, with guests who debate about world crises, economic predicaments, unpunished crime, and religious scandal, serious subjects for a thoughtful audience of diametrically opposed zealots. A prior day's homework in any subject will make you an expert who can hold her own with any authority."

"No question about that," said Phyllis.

"But I think you could also handle the earlier type of show, with its characteristic display of emotion, real or simulated. True, you can't produce tears, but even so . . ."

"I'm an experienced actress. I can represent any emotion that is called for by the part I play."

"Then what do you think, Phyl: personal calamities or international crises?"

"Let me watch both kinds of show, Ellery, so I am able to make an informed judgment."

"Ellery," Phyllis said eight days later, after a week of intensive application to the television screen, "my conclusion is that I should be better received by the potential audience if I had a daytime show dealing with issues of concern to the immediate lives of lower-middle-class persons individually, rather than those that apply to political entities, societies, nations, and planets, and here are my reasons: First and foremost, I am seen as being female, and women are commonly considered by human beings of both sexes as being more sensitive to emotional matters than are males, as men are thought to tend toward the analytical. Though many exceptions to the norm appear when any phase of human performance is studied closely, it is practical to work with averages when the purpose is to attract the public."

"Point well taken," said Pierce. "And you have more?"

"Secondly," Phyllis resumed, "while many women take part with confidence and authority in the evening discussions, great pains have been taken with their physical appearance—hair styles, jewelry, cosmetics, and attire. The same cannot be said about all the males, at least some of whom feel free to be unkempt, presumably because the audiences for these programs, persons of either sex, are relatively indifferent to the appearance of a man who expresses an opinion on an abstract matter, such as economic policy, that has no immediately measurable effect on a given individual."

"But you are as attractive as I could imagine," Pierce pointed out.

"Which can only distract from an issue at hand," said Phyllis, "unless, like the typical daytime subjects, it pertains to sex, in which case I should think the presence of a sexually desirable hostess might be an enhancement."

"Well thought out, Phyllis."

"There's more."

"Shoot." He chuckled at her frown. "That's an expression, having nothing to do with a gun."

"If you say so." She nodded briskly. "My third reason is that I would be better received by the TV audience in the role of sympathizer than as know-it-all."

16

Phyllis received some derision from the media, especially the late-night comics, but although her daily afternoon talk show, entitled *Phyllis from the Heart*, started slowly, by the end of a month and a half it claimed the lioness's share of the available TV audience for its time slot. There was general agreement among those who make such assessments that she brought a new style to the role. Not that either sentimentality or tough love was unprecedented, but her peculiar combination of the two, intermixed with or perhaps punctuated by a sudden suggestion of violence, kept audiences, at home and in the studio, on the razor's edge.

For example, when a big-bellied driver of an interstate eighteen-wheeler confessed to his wife that he regularly frequented truck-stop whores, Phyllis turned savagely on the woman.

"Isn't that how he first met *you?* And aren't you still turning tricks when he's on the road, you slut?"

"I'll be damn," said the truck driver, in his CAT-cap and plaid shirt. "I oughta kick your ass, you tramp."

"You just tell me, honey," Phyllis said to the wife. "If he touches you, I'll come and tear off his face."

The exclusively female audience sprang to its feet as one, with a cheer like cannonfire.

If a mother brought on her sullen teenaged son, whose chronic shoplifting supported his drug habit, Phyllis might well show apparent sympathy for the boy, telling the woman, "I'm going to send you home with a tape of this show, so you can study yourself and maybe see why any child of yours would want to stay permanently stoned."

But when the audience ended its clamor—pro and con, derisive hoots, enraged catcalls, gasps of uncertain empathy—Phyllis was likely to address the lad in a much sweeter tone. "Tony, despite all of your mother's concern for your well-being and the tens of thousands of dollars spent by the taxpayers to give you an education, you seem to be totally worthless. You'll probably spend most of your life in prison, being sodomized by the larger inmates, and unless you enjoy that sort of thing, you'll hang yourself in your cell. That's what is likely in store for you, but your coming here today to be publicly shamed means that at least you have an exhibitionistic vanity, which suggests that your instincts for survival are not quite as dead as the rest of your wretched self. So you still have some hope, however tiny, of making it if you get in one of the programs on the list you will be given backstage. And if your mother wants, we will follow your progress until, as is probable, you foul it up as usual."

In some quarters Phyllis was criticized for her approach, but the results were often positive. Tony, for example, was still doing all right, half a year afterward, as were several other adolescent sometime delinquents, members of criminal gangs, juvenile sex predators, arsonists; but after a catfight on Phyllis's show, a sixteen-year-old named Kellianne tried to poison a rival for a place on the cheerleading squad, and both the victim's parents and Kellianne's sued the program. As did the formerly brutal gay-basher who as a result of his appearance on Phyllis's show underwent a radical transformation and took a homosexual lover, owing to which liaison he allegedly became HIV-positive.

Then too, Phyllis was the defendant in a lawsuit brought by a man who had stalked her for months before making his move in the studio parking lot, a few yards ahead of the bodyguards entertainment celebrities are obliged to maintain to ward off homicidal cranks, as she walked to the stretch limo inside which Pierce awaited her, cell phone at his ear as usual.

"How dare you ignore my love letters?" the stalker cried, breaking through the security detail that restrained the crowd of autograph-seekers, brandishing a twelve-inch knife of the type that had been sheathed on the leopard-skin thong worn by Phyllis in her action films.

Though it had been some time now since she had made such a movie, Phyllis had necessarily remained, without working out, in the same superb condition as when she had performed her own stunts. She caught the descending blade just above its keen edge and snapped it off the hilt while backhanding the attacker with sufficient force to knock out most of his front teeth.

At Pierce's direction, the publicity people managed to keep news of this incident out of the media. He believed the time was still not ripe for revealing Phyllis's true identity, which such a demonstration of superhuman physical prowess might call into question. In the interests of this strategy, the madman's lawyer was granted a generous settlement, and the nut went free no doubt to menace others, but hey, that was their lookout. Since becoming a show-biz *macher*, Pierce had acquired a cynicism quite foreign to the lonely applied-scientist he had been in his earlier life, before Phyllis had exceeded his most extravagant dreams.

They were wealthy now, he and she, and growing richer through the packaging deals, commercial endorsements, website sales of tie-in merchandise, videos, action figures, coffee mugs, T-shirts, and the like, in all of which Pierce was prime mover, amazing himself by his accomplishment in the new métier.

"Who would have ever suspected I could do well as a businessman?" he asked Phyllis once when they were alone, for he knew well enough never to have asked it of anyone else.

"You can do anything you wish."

"I don't think it's wise to confuse our respective capabilities, Phyl. *You're* the one with unlimited potential. I'm only human."

"By which you mean you will die?"

"That's not a real question. But aging, terminating in mortality, is not my only limitation."

"Well, there you have one of mine," Phyllis said. "I cannot understand that statement."

For all Phyllis's remarkable talents, she was like a little child in assuming her begetter was omnipotent. But only with regard to Pierce was she naïve. Her series of self-help books was endorsed by many professionals as being compendia of principles and practices of tough but benevolent good sense. "Self-pity is a denial of self." "Don't do good. Always do better." "If you debate whether giving is preferable to receiving, or vice versa, you are wasting your life." "Decent manners should be irrelevant to personal tastes." Such aphorisms came easily to Phyllis, who dictated her books at conversational speed to a voice-generated word processor that Pierce, keeping his hand in the technology arena, did not invent but improved considerably.

On the commercial success of her first book, Phyllis agreed to furnish a monthly column to *Herself*, the leading women's magazine, and these were collected periodically into paperback volumes that were displayed on supermarket checkout racks, near the sensation-mongering tabloids that for years had failed to find anything scandalous to allege about her, though surely they must have tried. Something about Phyllis, some obvious, seemingly congenital purity of character, along with her social reclusiveness, had kept her immune from hostile scrutiny. And thus far no disgruntled ex-employees had surfaced, for she had always insisted that Pierce be generous to those who worked for them, with high salaries, bonuses, and costly gifts—often against his objection—not owing to emotional motives that she could not have, but rather because it was rational to reward people consonant with the income from the business, which in Phyllis's case was now enormous, so much so in fact that eventually her chief accountant was emboldened to embezzle a million and a half. On discovering this crime Pierce intended to send him to prison, but Phyllis said no, the money could be declared advance payment of his wages, which he would subsequently pay back by faithful service to those who had kept him a free man.

"Phyllis," Pierce said one day, "I do nothing but work, and while it is gratifying to have such success and I'm not complaining, this isn't the field I had originally chosen for myself, and my responsibilities have taken their toll."

"Ellery," said she, "as I have told you every time you make

that point, why don't you delegate to others some of the tasks that are less rewarding?"

"Because I don't trust anyone else."

"I could fend for myself if you want some time off. Perhaps go to Hawaii, lie on the beach, enjoying tropical drinks."

"You can't swim, and you shouldn't even get near any sand," Pierce pointed out. "Some of it might work its way into your systems, however careful you are."

"I don't need rest or recreation. Take along a girl who likes to swim and sunbathe, and have sex with her. See if there's anything I could do better. But I would advise not taking any of the young women who work for us, lest she subsequently become overbearing."

Such suggestions made Pierce despondent, welcome as they might have been if voiced by his human wives or even a girlfriend of more than six months' duration. Fabricating his own woman had certainly paid off for him, in more ways than one, but that there was a tax on his emotions could not be denied. By so blithely urging him to be unfaithful to her, Phyllis only reminded him of her own moral neutrality. It was but an absence of sexual desire that kept her out of other men's beds. He had to accept that state of affairs, because it was he who had made her that way. Her extramarital chastity was due to *him*, not Phyllis.

In the lowest of moments he was capable of seeing her as essentially the realization of a masturbatory fantasy. But then she would do something so delightfully surprising as to distract him from soul-searching. After viewing a DVD of *Rain Man*, she reproduced the idiot-savant feats of Dustin Hoffman's character, counting the individual matches in a boxful while they fell en masse to the floor; reproducing from memory the names, addresses, and numbers in a telephone directory after one quick perusal thereof; identifying each playing card in a deck that was scattered before her at high speed—all without a concomitant show of autistic disabilities.

"Perhaps you could make a valuable contribution to psychiatric research, Phyl."

"I'll get started on that immediately, Ellery."

She was heading for the nearest computer when he called her back. "But not quite yet. It would mean revealing what you are. It's still not time for that."

He had nobody with whom to discuss the matter but her. "You might well wonder what I'm waiting for—I know you don't, but indulge me in this. From the moment you are revealed to be a product of technology and not of nature, it will be a different ballgame—uh, situation."

"I understand the term in this context," Phyllis said. "'Ballgame' is the *mot juste*. You can't know what will happen when the shit hits the fan."

After Pierce fell asleep at night, she watched contemporary movies, with their obscene dialogue, on cable. There was no purpose in feigning a sleep she did not require, so long as she was beside him when he awakened next morning.

"I—we have to be prepared," said he. "But just *how* I haven't yet been able to decide. Will the public be outraged or amused or favorably impressed? Maybe all three, though as it stands I think the third is least likely. There are people who will feel betrayed, made fools of, especially those who have relied on your advice since the TV show went on the air. The previous movies don't concern me: nonhuman heroes seem natural to action films. Look at video games—and by the way, yours are still near the top in sales after several years."

"Maybe I should start right away to solve the problem of autism," Phyllis said.

"I don't know." Pierce put his fingers to his temples. "My head is spinning, Phyl."

"You need a vacation, Ellery. That's obvious. Before you have a nervous breakdown, whatever that is."

Instructing Phyllis always momentarily relieved the strain on him for which she was generally responsible. "It's an old-fashioned term, Phyl. Today the word is 'stress.'"

"The beaches of the French Riviera are covered with pebbles rather than sand," Phyllis told him. "I could sit on a chair and read while you swim."

"Why are you intent on getting me into the water, Phyl?"

"Because water is the element most fundamental to the human condition, and bathing in it is universally considered therapeutic and regenerative for many complaints of body and mind."

"My mother taught me to swim." Pierce smiled in nostalgia. "In a hotel pool. She was a Vegas showgirl."

"You've never mentioned that before."

"What would it have mattered to you, Phyl?"

Phyllis frowned. "To be sure, I don't have a bloodtie to your mother, but we do share a tradition."

"In her heyday my mother was blonde and five feet ten. She was primarily a dancer, but she could sing well, too. You are not a mother-substitute, Phyllis."

"You seem overly sensitive on that subject, Ellery. I do believe you are suffering from stress and should take a vacation. Of course I'll come along if you wish. There's always plenty for me to do so long as I have access to TV and the internet."

"All that remains is the choice of destination. How about

Europe? The Houses of Parliament, the Eiffel Tower, Vatican City, the Kremlin. Or Asia: the Ginza, the Great Wall, the Raffles Hotel, the Taj Mahal?"

"Kuala Lumpur, site of the tallest buildings in the world."

"Think of the information you'll acquire on the spot," Pierce said, "expanding even further your range of reference." He suddenly smacked himself on the forehead. "Damn! I forgot all about the checkers at the airline gates. You've got too much metal in you to clear the machine. And you'd get special attention as a celebrity. Any search would be ruinous."

"You don't mean literally, I believe, but rather with reference to your intention to keep my identity under wraps. I'm sorry, Ellery."

"It's not your fault."

"'What would you have me be, an I be not a woman?' *Pericles*, by William Shakespeare, Act Four, Scene Two, line eighty-four."

Pierce spoke tenderly. "The problem here is not that you're a woman, Phyl, but because you're artificial."

"I gather it hasn't occurred to you that we are prosperous enough to charter a plane or, even more conveniently, purchase one for our exclusive use."

He chuckled. "Right you are, Phyl, as always. I still haven't gotten used to living on this level." They now owned a mansion even larger and more luxurious than that which Phyllis had occupied as an action-film star, with a staff of appropriate size and a number of automobiles, all chauffeur-driven, for Pierce was too busy to drive and though Phyllis could have learned to operate a motor vehicle in a matter of minutes, she did not do so because that would have been unseemly for a celebrity of her magnitude.

So Pierce put his people on to the matter of a private airplane, and soon Phyllis, Inc. had its own Learjet, the cost of which of course could be written off as a business expense. But before it could be used for Pierce's badly needed vacation, Phyllis was invited to dinner at the White House by the President of the United States.

17

Tell you the truth, Phyllis—may I call you Phyllis?—the official reason for inviting you here is your generous support of children's charities, which as you know is the issue the First Lady cares most about—well, that is, after the general well-being of the country." President Joe Sloan lifted his square jaw, shook his head of carefully tousled, copper-red hair, and winked a heavy-lidded eye. "You wanna know my real reason?"

Phyllis had been coached at length by Pierce for this encounter. "Yes, Mr. President."

"You cain't guess?"

"No, Mr. President."

"I was the Numero Uno fan of your movies." He leered at her. "Darn if I wasn't. It just tickled me to see a little gal whip some great big fella. I don't know why, maybe because I worshipped my mama, who was just a little bitty peanut of a person but had a giant-sized personality, and had to have one to handle my daddy and four brothers—count 'em, five of us—in a mobile home with an old Chevy up on blocks in the side yard, dirt poor, but there wasn't any shortage of love. Now, are you a mama yourself, Phyllis?"

"No, Mr. President."

"Maybe I should speak to your hubby about that matter, whadduh yuh think? I contend a woman should have all she's got comin'. I'm known for that position. I notice you made short work of that turtle soup. I approve of a lady with a good appetite. Down where I come from, that's no detriment like it is up East with them snobs like my daddy used to call 'em. They cain't deal with a real woman. You like those cheese straws?"

"Yes, Mr. President."

"The First Lady had all our four children in a row, back when I was a backwoods lawyer, got that out of the way so to speak. They were pretty much grown up by my second term in the Senate. Two of them are married now and one turned Muslim, damn if she didn't, God bless her. The fourth is taking her masters in hotel management at Cornell. Her substance-abuse problem is a thing of the past." He touched Phyllis's wrist just above the diamond-and-sapphire bracelet Pierce had put there. "I'm runnin' on about myself. Let's talk about that killer TV show of yours. Let me give you a suggestion. Invite the First Lady as an on-air guest. You choose the subject. She majored in astrophysics as an undergraduate at Cal Tech, then switched to sinology and went to Harvard grad school. She's fluent in Mandarin, for pity sake, and talked the arm off the Chinese ambassador in his own lingo. Phew, too rich for my blood. I mean the truffle sauce on this filly, give me plain porterhouse with nothin' but salt, side of sliced tomata and Bermuda onion. Down where I come from, they'll take a dill pickle, dip it in batter, and deep-fry that sucker. Ever tasted one of them?"

Pierce was seated at another table, next to Amber Sloan, the wife of the President of the United States.

"It looks like my husband is having an absorbing conversation with Mrs. Pierce," said she.

"Yes, doesn't it?" Pierce replied. "Phyllis is a great admirer of his policies." He smiled blandly toward their dinner companions around the table, the U.S. ambassador to a minuscule country in Latin America, his glittering wife, campaign contributors from big business and big labor, and an affable Asian who spoke English with a British accent.

"What are my chances of appearing on her show?" asked the First Lady, a plump woman of a certain age, with bronze-colored hair and a generous mouth, but mean little eyes even when enhanced heavily with liner and purple shadow.

"I'll put in a good word," Pierce said, "insofar as I have any influence."

That was said in levity, but Amber Sloan frowned. "I understood you were executive producer."

"I am, of course," he hastened to say. "When would you like to come on?"

"Call my appointments secretary." Having crisply said which, Mrs. Sloan turned to speak, in a more ingratiating manner, to the very pink-faced, white-sideburned man on her right, a mogul of high finance.

Pierce got his chance to compare notes with Phyllis only at a moment during the dancing that followed dinner, President Sloan having monopolized her company all evening thus far.

"Looks like you and the Chief Executive have been hitting it off, Phyl. Where'd he go?"

"He told me he had to leave for a minute to start a war, Ellery," said Phyllis, a vision in form-fitting silver lamé.

"I imagine he was joking," Pierce said. "As I told you, he is known for his sense of humor. It looked to me like your worries about not being able to dance well were groundless."

"It helps that the President is not a very good dancer himself. He just hugs me and shuffles around."

They were standing at the side of the chandeliered ballroom, near a snowy-naperied table holding a crystal punchbowl presided over by a solemn male functionary in White House livery.

"I know it can't mean anything to you, Phyl," Pierce said, looking at the resplendent assemblage of gowns and tailcoats, "but speaking as an American who never in his wildest dreams could imagine being a guest in this place, I am thrilled to the bone. And I owe it all to you."

"Then it was worth your while to have created me. Is that what you are saying, Ellery?"

"I certainly am, Phyl. You've made me wealthy and given me access to power. If you were human, I'd be a gigolo and I'd probably resent you for doing all this for me. My male pride couldn't take it."

"Ellery, the President presses an erection against me when we dance."

"*Shh*, Phyllis." Pierce drew her away from a man approaching the punchbowl. He spoke sotto voce. "Don't acknowledge it in any way."

"He's got a name for it."

"Keep your voice down!"

She whispered, "He says he wants me to shake hands with Little Joe."

"He's a great kidder, Phyl. He's famous for his jokes."

"Am I supposed to fuck him, Ellery? He *is* commander-in-chief of the greatest array of military power the world has ever known, so he says."

"That's true enough. But no, you don't have to have sex with him. You're my wife."

"He told me to tell you that in exchange you can fuck *his* wife."

"No thanks."

"What he wants is for me to rough him up, as I did to the villains in my movies. I can't convince him it was only acting."

Pierce glanced around. The man at the punchbowl wore a broad red ribbon across his shirtfront and a row of multicolored decorations on the left breast. Pierce's own tailcoat was unadorned except for a white carnation. He could probably earn a Presidential honor by letting Joe Sloan have his way with Phyllis, but at least he was above that.

"The simplest thing would be just to leave before he gets back."

"But you are enjoying yourself, Ellery. I could kick the President's ass if that's what he wants."

"If the media found out about that, and they always do with this guy, it wouldn't be good for the business. We've got to keep your image clean."

Phyllis nodded her head toward the orchestra on the dais. "Ellery, have you noticed who has the second chair in the reed section?"

"That's quite a distance away, and I don't have your vision, Phyl."

"Do you remember Tyler Hallstrom?"

"You must be in error. He's probably a lookalike." Pierce squinted. He was not getting any younger. "What would Hallstrom be doing here?"

"Obviously he's been programmed to play the saxophone," Phyllis said.

"I wonder why that isn't the Marine band."

"President Sloan told me he prefers civilian orchestras, to get away from the military connotation."

Pierce did not really remember Hallstrom that clearly. Some years had passed since he last saw that animatronic personage, at the time Cliff Pulsifer's significant other. "Maybe the whole band is robotic, Phyl, like the one in those old horror movies of Vincent Price's."

"The *Dr. Phibes* series," she said promptly. "But they were caricatures. All the other musicians here are human."

"You can tell that without closer inspection?"

"It takes one to know one," said she. She looked past him. "Uh-oh, here comes the President, Ellery."

Sloan had a style of intruding on the personal space of people he spoke with while standing. His height was only average if that, but his intimidating geniality made him seem larger. "How you doin', El? I been looking for an opportunity to get our heads together. A fella like yourself who has cobbled together an entertainment empire oughta be able to provide some good ideas for government. My people'll be in touch. Meanwhile, the President of the United States is gonna claim the company of your beautiful wife again, if you don't mind." He came even closer, virtually laying his red head on Pierce's shoulder to whisper, breath smelling of saltines, "Use my private crapper if you want to take a dump or just drain the lizard, escorted by the Secret Service. Tell 'em I said so. Hope I didn't use up the last of the ass-wipe with Ransome's picture on it. You'll get a kick outta that."

Sloan was running for reelection against a Midwestern governor named Jack Ransome, a man of gravity as opposed to the buffoonishness for which the former was celebrated by those whose primary need was entertainment, whereas Ransome bored even his own adherents with long humorless speeches that tended rather to obscure than elucidate the issues. The incumbent had a lead in the polls, but he had not reached the highest office in the land by neglecting any opportunity. Pierce had never been much of a partisan political man, but he was well aware that the success of Phyllis's talk show made her support worth acquiring, and it was as typical of Sloan to cultivate it as for Ransome to neglect to do so.

With mixed feelings Pierce watched as Sloan glued himself to Phyllis and shuffled away with her, the throng on the dance floor parting respectfully to give them clearance. Pierce felt like a pimp, but he was also swollen by a kind of afflatus. Being in the presence of a President, even one who had toilet paper imprinted with an image of his opponent, in the edifice that was the center of the known universe, was a unique and exalting experience.

"The First Lady would like you to ask her for a dance," said a feminine voice at his elbow.

He turned to see an owlishly eyeglassed young woman in a modest, even dowdy evening gown of the sort worn by ladies-in-waiting in a democratic court. She led him around the edge of the floor to where Amber Sloan sat surrounded by other retainers.

"May I be so bold," Pierce asked obsequiously, "as to ask you to dance with me?"

Mrs. Sloan was slow to acquiesce, first looking away, smirking as if in disdain. Then she gave him a hostile stare before her lips parted in a wide, almost carnivorous smile. "Why," said she, rising, "I thought you'd never ask." At which her cohorts, a mixture of sexes, politely haha-ed in unison.

"Please forgive me in advance," Pierce said. "I haven't danced in years."

"My people tell me," said the First Lady, "that you and Phyllis are not very social for show folks. We'd like to see you at some Party fund-raisers."

Pierce was trying to concentrate on not stepping on her toes as they box-stepped to a Broadway show tune, the melody of which was familiar to all but only the superannuated could have named. "That's true," said he. "We work so hard that in our rare moments of time off we treasure our privacy."

"Well now," said Amber Sloan, whose plump, faintly freckled cleavage Pierce noticed for the first time as he almost stumbled, "that's a chickenshit excuse if I ever heard one." But she displayed one of her toothiest grins. She was a tough one to figure out.

Pierce heard himself say, "We'll do better in the future, I promise."

The First Lady cocked her head, favoring one piercing green eye. "I'll hold you to it, Ellery, count on it. What you *don't* have to do is let Phyllis go down on Joe. I promise he won't sic the IRS on you."

"That's nice to know." Pierce managed to speak as though this sort of exchange was routine, as perhaps it was on the upper levels of power.

By now, without conscious direction, at least on his part—he led but seemed nevertheless to be under the control of the President's wife—they had danced near Sloan and Phyllis.

"Hi there, neighbors!" the Chief Executive cried. "I haven't enjoyed myself so much since the last time I ate a bowl of possum gumbo. How about this band? Just don't ask them to play anything more recent than the '50s. But that's who you gotta have if you invite *alter kockers* like the Chief Justice and the Majority Whip."

Pierce was now close enough to the orchestra to discern that Phyllis had been correct: One of the saxophonists indeed seemed to be Tyler Hallstrom, who of course had not changed at all in appearance while acquiring a new skill, which in a creature of his type meant new programming. Phyllis could have been given a sense of rhythm and an ability to dance like a prima ballerina assoluta were Pierce to take the trouble. That he did not was due to his own deficiencies in that area, to correct which he could have done little.

Hallstrom now rose from his chair, presumably to perform one of those solos of the big-band era. Like his colleagues he wore a navy-blue blazer with an embroidered breast-pocket badge.

He came to the edge of the dais, shoving the remonstrating leader aside. While en route, he had pulled his sax apart and reassembled it into a multibarreled automatic weapon. He fired a burst into one of the chandeliers, which snowed chunks of crystal onto the cringing statesmen and their screaming ladies on the dance floor, and afterward shouted in a voice that had undoubtedly been enhanced electronically to be stentorian: "There is but one God and Mohammed is his prophet!"

President Sloan quickly ducked behind Phyllis, but his wife strode past Pierce to say, in stern schoolmarm style, "You just put that gun down before someone gets hurt."

Hallstrom continued to look into the middle distance while apparently responding to the First Lady. "Silence, dirty Western slut, or you die!"

"Now, you just listen here—" She was quickly surrounded by Secret Service agents, who had been in discreet attendance on her and her husband all evening, never far away though so unobtrusive as to have been all but invisible to Pierce until this moment.

They had also moved to screen the President, which would have meant Phyllis as well, for he was still clutching her, had she not broken away and approached the bandstand.

"Tyler, do you remember me?"

Hallstrom fired another burst at what was left of the nearest chandelier, while the screams of the assemblage were modulated to sobs.

"Defilers of the shrines," he cried. "There will be sorrow in your tents."

"Knock off that Islamist shit, Tyler," Phyllis said quietly. "You're just a dumb robot who's picked up some slogans he doesn't understand."

"Infidel whore!"

"Give me the gun, Tyler." She extended her hand.

As Hallstrom stared at her, his expression changed from the vacant aspect of terrorist self-righteousness to melancholy reproach. "We could have had something, Phyllis. If only you had not been corrupted by the secular materialists."

"It's not too late yet," said she and, lifting the constraining skirt of the lamé gown to mid-thigh, she leaped gracefully onto the dais beside him.

Pierce sought the shelter of the crowd. He was suddenly more afraid *of* Phyllis than *for* her.

"I must first kill the mendacious and hypocritical adulterer who leads the Great Satan," Hallstrom said. "Then we will go away together." He pointed the Gatling barrels of the transformed saxophone at the cluster of Secret Service personnel surrounding the President and would surely have begun to fire had not Phyllis, using as handle a hunk of the blond hair, opened a panel in the back of his head and with one crooked finger pulled loose a sheaf of wires.

Though a stalwart figure only a second earlier, Hallstrom now collapsed onto himself as if being disassembled. His eyelids stayed wide open, however, and his big flaxen head, now between his upturned feet, displayed a frozen blue stare, his mouth curved in a faint smile.

The ring of agents parted to allow the Chief Executive to emerge. He was helped to mount the bandstand while some of the Secret Service agents carried Hallstrom's body away and others examined the machine-gun sax.

Sloan raised both arms in triumph and accepted the applause of the crowd. As was his specialty, he transformed, at least for this collection of partisans, what might have been seen as a weakness into a strength. "I don't mind admitting I had quite a scare. I'm only human." He pointed at the crotch of his black evening trousers, which those standing close enough could see was damp. He made a hooting laugh. "I dropped a glass of punch on myself! . . . But how about this plucky little woman?" He gestured toward Phyllis. "I'm also mighty proud of my wife. Didja see how she stepped forward? Let's have a hand for the ladies, God blessum."

18

Joe Sloan's poll numbers had begun to slip even before the blockbusting revelation came. People really did not consider it a joke that a President of the United States, even when in apparent danger of losing his life, would piss his pants.

The decline in popularity was so sudden and so precipitous that those who ran his campaign began to panic. Though he himself did not share this feeling, Sloan had always been able unerringly to gauge when to defy one's staff and when to give in to them, as he was famous for his ability to get away with outrageous stunts that would have destroyed the career of anyone else (flatulating loudly during one state-of-the-union address, then revealing, to the stunned House and the TV cameras, the little rubber-bulb fart simulator concealed in his left hand; goosing the Chinese ambassador as they returned from a walk at Camp David; appointing a gay Secretary of State, to whom he ascribed "Swish" descent, "but don't ask William Tell," which caused the Alpine nation temporarily to recall their ambassador in protest).

But now he had committed two rare lapses in judgment. The assassination attempt, his own idea, had been a fake. Hallstrom's weapon was loaded with blanks, the chandelier wired with the explosive "squibs" used in movies. An animatron had been chosen for the job so that the Secret Service agents could shoot it down with impunity. That a Phyllis would intervene had not been imagined; that playing a lovable coward would not prove ingratiating, even with a public insatiable for amusement, had not been considered.

Sloan's second mistake was to acquiesce in his advisors' urgent, perhaps even hysterical plea that he take emergency measures to halt his snowballing negatives. He was of course too rational to consider calling for the complete abolition of the personal income tax or the annexation of Canada, but it was, again, his own initiative that had unforeseen, and unfortunate, consequences.

"Foreskin," he announced at the next strategy meeting, addressing Vice President Dean Forsythe, a sixty-seven-year-old political hack who had been originally chosen for, and had thoroughly lived up to, a deprivation in luster, "I sure hate to do this, old buddy, but you're gonna have to step off the ticket. I'm gonna name Phyllis Pierce for V.P."

Forsythe showed an unprecedented spirit. "That showbiz bitch? Joe, you've finally gone too far, you prick."

"I *knew* you'd give your all for the party," Sloan said with enthusiasm and the genuine affection he felt for those he betrayed. "Let's hear it for Foreskin!" He led the applause.

———

Pierce considered the proposal for less than a day before what should be done became clear.

"Phyllis," said he, "if you are qualified to be vice president, you are qualified to be president."

"That would seem to be true," said she.

"It will require a write-in campaign, and we've got less than a year. But I think we can maybe just pull it off."

"Ellery, does that mean I have to leave show business?"

"Were you to stay on the show, by law the opposition would have to be given equal time. But you'll be on the air a lot, making public appearances and in political commercials. That will require quite as much simulated emotion as *The Lady of the Camellias*. You'll be exercising all of your skills, I promise you. Politics *is* showbiz and sometimes it's even more lucrative though usually less believable." Pierce often nowadays amazed himself with his clear grasp of reality, but he was well aware that he could never have developed this skill had he not created Phyllis as an ideal.

"Have you decided yet," she asked, "when you'll reveal my true identity, or lack thereof?"

"That's still puzzling. All that's certain is that now is definitely not yet the right time. The tremendous boost you are enjoying for having handled Hallstrom—who so far as you presumably knew was a dangerous terrorist—would be largely nullified were it known that you yourself are simply another animatron. Nobody wants a wimpy leader, male or female—Sloan must be losing his grip to pull this stunt—but a machine is another matter. I think you'd be the first to admit that courage did not come into play."

"You do not speak with a forked tongue, Ellery."

Pierce squinted at her. "Do I hear some new irony, Phyl? I thought that was impossible. Or did you watch an old Western last night, with Hollywood Indians?"

"The latter," said Phyllis. "I was quoting."

"We'll begin immediately to work on your political image. That's too big a job for me alone. We'll have to hire a team of professionals, and they don't come cheap, nor does TV time, travel, and all the other expenses. No matter how much money is raised, all campaigns pile up debts that never get fully paid off. Sloan still owes for his first one, and his contributors include some of the richest in the country—corporations, big unions, and professional associations. Some of the same also give money to Ransome, in addition to which he has a huge personal fortune. We used to seem rich, Phyl, but we aren't in this context. So we have to start grass-roots fund-raising immediately."

"I'm ready to work twenty-four seven."

"Reminds me," said Pierce, "to be on the safe side, I'm going to give you a complete overhaul this weekend. Time to replace your batteries again; they've been recharged enough." He had already done this once during her stressful efforts to get reestablished in show business. It was something of an emotional ordeal for him to see Phyllis in effect dead during the time it took to effect the change, all her systems disconnected, open eyes staring without focus if he had neglected to tell her to close them before the current was switched off, not a lifeless body but rather a mechanical device that had ceased to function, nevertheless dismaying to him who loved her.

———

It was during Phyllis's overhauling, in Pierce's secret workshop behind the locked ex–wine cellar door, that a servant summoned him by intercom to take an important phone call upstairs.

"How they hangin', El?" asked President Joe Sloan, who assumed his strident tenor and border accent provided self-identification. "Putcha lady on, if you don't mind."

"Phyllis is indisposed at the moment, Mr. President."

"Tell her to get off the pot, pronto. This is the President of the United States."

"She's medicated," said Pierce. "She was a bit under the weather and the doctor—"

"Fuck that shit," Sloan said, losing his geniality. "I was supposed to get an answer back by today about that thing under consideration."

"As to the vice presidency," Pierce began.

"Hush!" Sloan ordered. "I'm told you ain't got a secure phone."

"As to the matter that your assistant, Jim Max—"

"Goddammit," cried the Chief Executive. "I'm not gonna tell you a third time."

"The thing under consideration, then. With all respect, and every acknowledgment of the honor bestowed by the very proposal, Phyllis must decline."

"Why, you little turd," Sloan shouted. "I want to talk to Phyllis personally, else the FBI's gonna kick down your door and search for the kiddie porn I hear you collect."

"Before they arrive, the entire media will have the real story, Mr. President."

Sloan was instantly contrite. "Now don't tell me a smart fella like yourself don't reckanize a joke when he hears one,

Ellery, for pity sake. I just would appreciate the courtesy of a call from Phyllis when she feels up to it. I think I got that much comin', don't you?"

"Of course, Mr. President. She'll get back to you as soon as she has recovered her faculties."

"I sure hope that's not as bad as it sounds."

Sloan was known as a blusterer, but as it was also true that he had many sorts of weapons at his disposal, including the IRS, Pierce thought it unwise to keep him in the dark too long about their plans. It would be safer to be his declared political adversaries, thereby becoming too conspicuous to be victims of the dirtiest tricks.

So the overhaul did not get quite as much time as would have been optimum, but when Phyllis's power supply was replaced and fully operational, she made the call to the White House.

Sloan began with solicitousness and flattery, but when he heard from Phyllis's own lips that not only did she reject the vice-presidential offer but would run against him for the top office, he lost his famous temper and spouted obscenities, concluding with, "I'll whup your ass, bitch," a phrase that became the favorite one-liner of the campaign when Pierce provided the tape to the media.

Cliff Pulsifer still lived where he had when Pierce had last seen him, at dinner that evening, years before, when Cliff kindly provided his sister as solace.

"Ellery," Cliff said now, taking both his hands and giving him an intense stare. "You don't look a day older."

Pierce lyingly said the same thing about Cliff, who however had acquired a lot of gray at the temples, purplish bags under his eyes, and a very pasty complexion.

"I'm afraid I don't drink any more," Cliff said, leading him into the living room, "but I can offer several flavors of Snapple."

Pierce took the proffered chair. "I won't waste your valuable time, Cliff. Let me tell you why I came: Hallstrom." And when Cliff looked blank, "Tyler Hallstrom? . . . The so-called attempted assassination of President Sloan?"

"Oh, *that*," said Pulsifer. "Yes, I heard of that." He smirked quickly. "I'll admit it, Ellery, I've been at a detox center, getting clean. I was out of it for a while. I'm just getting back on my feet. Couldn't have done it without Alicia's help. She's an angel."

"How *is* your sister?" Pierce asked ritualistically, then went on without waiting for a response. "I've hit rock bottom myself, in my time. Do you remember Phyllis?" He brought Cliff up to date, which took a while even though Pierce dealt only with the highlights, for there were great gaps. For example, though Cliff was dimly aware of a cult-film star named Phyllis, he had had no suspicion she was one and the same as Pierce's wife. And in fact, for a moment or two, he had some difficulty in recalling that the latter Phyllis had been animatronic.

"I'm still not up to snuff, Ellery, forgive me. I've been unlucky in love, of course. But who isn't, when it comes to that? Only, not everybody develops chemical dependencies."

"But that night I came to dinner here and met your sister," Pierce asked, "you had broken up with, I think the name was Ray? You had a new companion."

"A tall blond?" Cliff grimaced into the middle distance. "He didn't stay long. He was just a brief stop on my way downhill. Taylor something, or something Taylor."

"Tyler Hallstrom," Pierce said. "The guy who last week supposedly tried to assassinate the President."

"You're pulling my leg. Forgive me, I haven't watched the news that carefully. My God. He was *here?* I gave lodging to a terrorist?"

"He too was an animatron."

"I had a much longer relationship with Ray. He's the one I knew best." Cliff whewed, looking more dismal than ever. "I had a close call."

"Incidentally, what became of Ray?"

"His next lover had him dismantled, I heard. He could be impossible."

Pierce took Cliff into his confidence as to the matter of Phyllis's bid for the presidency. "It's essential for now that her identity not be revealed. You're one of the few human beings who could reveal it. Now, if I'm asking for your discretion, I don't do so empty-handed. When Phyllis is President, we intend to establish a permanent liaison to the gay community. I see a place for you."

Cliff smiled wanly. "I really don't know if I'd be up to it, Ellery, but it's sweet of you to make the offer. Don't worry about my blabbing. I promise you I won't. Nobody'd believe me anyway, at this point."

"Well, I won't forget you, Cliff," Pierce said, rising. "Let me know if I can help in any fashion. I hope you meet someone soon."

"God forbid!" Cliff gasped. "That's the source of all my troubles. I'm *trying* to pry my heart off my sleeve, at this late date."

———

Janet formerly Hallstrom was a more difficult case. First it took Pierce's private investigators a while to locate her. She was no longer surnamed Hallstrom. She had disposed of her business some years before and apparently left town, but for where was not easy to determine. It became evident that she was intentionally dodging her creditors.

When she was finally run to ground, it turned out she had not moved far at all. She had remained local, but simply had altered her name to Janet Stromhall, which was enough to make her legally invisible.

It had been Phyllis's suggestion that the tracers consider such a transposition of syllables. "It's one of a number of simple cryptological procedures, Ellery, but effective sometimes when the adversary expects more sophisticated techniques."

In distinction to Cliff, Janet was well aware of Hallstrom's recent exploit and was deliberating on the possibilities of profiting from it in some way, as she readily admitted to Pierce when he found her.

"Look," she said, "Phyllis was making it big time in the movies at just the point where my own fortunes began to fall. Then came the TV show. Now she's some kind of heroine, and running for President? Give me a break! A goddam robot? Who does she think she is?"

"When we get into office," Pierce assured her, "we're setting up a special department of the Small Business Administration devoted to women. That'll need to be headed up by someone who knows what she wants. I see a big role for you."

But this was not quite enough to ensure Janet's cooperation. "I'm trying to get back in business, Ellery, but I'm underfunded."

He chewed his lip. "That's our problem too, Janet. We started the campaign late, all the major contributors were already taken. We're having to go to the little guy with twenty-dollar bills."

"My heart bleeds," Janet said, "but for myself. I'm having a tough time just paying the phone bill, not to mention the office rent."

"I'll see what we can do, Janet."

19

It went without saying that had Phyllis been human she could not have run for President at that late a date, the demands of a campaign being what they were physically, emotionally, psychically, nor could Pierce have played any role at all. As it was, he drew his strength from her, she who had an inexhaustible supply thereof, as well as a wisdom that he was tempted nonsensically to call natural; it compensated for his utter lack of experience in politics.

Of course they had a full complement of hired advisors, among them several of Joe Sloan's former aides, since disaffected by his reflex action when in trouble, viz, to shitjob the nearest at hand (e.g., the Commerce Secretary who repeated to a reporter a fat-woman joke told him by Sloan; the general who on Sloan's demand let the President operate the remote controls of a drone aircraft that subsequently plunged into the Caribbean only narrowly missing a crowded cruise ship; the gay assistant whom Sloan used as "beard" during the latter's affair with the teenaged daughter of Biff Oakland, the movie star and Sloan crony: The secretary was fired, the general lost a star, and Jameson Webb sustained a beating from Oakland that put him in the hospital).

Webb was eager to furnish extensive data on Sloan's illicit sexual exploits, and there were those, Pierce among them, who were keen on using such in a campaign that everyone assumed must go negative if it were to overcome the disadvantages of a late start, an inexperienced candidate, and the write-in process.

But it was Phyllis who, at first single-handedly, opposed this policy. "It might be otherwise if there were only one or two examples," said she, "and furthermore if they had been hitherto unknown to the general electorate, or at least only the fare of supermarket tabloids. But President Sloan is famous for such episodes, which have been so frequent as to become a joke. And in fact, if the phony assassination attempt is indicative, there may be reason to believe that some of these events have been cut from the whole cloth by Joe Sloan himself."

"But why, Phyllis," Pierce asked, speaking for most of the others around the strategy table, "would he defame himself?"

"Obviously, he went too far with the fake assassination, but up to now, such tactics have usually worked very well. There are many human beings who feel better about themselves if they think they are morally superior to those above them in power or wealth. Sloan early on learned an effective means to allay envy. His opponent last time was too impeccable to be attractive to most people, whom he made feel inferior: teetotaling, ethically stainless, a war hero whose apparent purpose as a civilian business success was to become a philanthropist. Sloan saw that he could hardly compete with Wellington in virtue. His only hope was as a scoundrel—not an outright criminal but someone just contemptible enough to amuse a plurality of the voters in a time of peace."

It was old Howell Fairchild, veteran of three Presidential campaigns—two of them victorious—who asked, "The latest stunt was a bridge too far?"

"*Cowardly* is what most people regard as natural. *Being* a coward is unacceptable."

Old Fairchild nodded respectfully. He had not gotten to be the dean of campaign advisors by disregarding intelligent analysis from whatever source, and he soon recognized in Phyllis, though she had come from the vast nullity, to him, of the realm outside politics, a brilliant young woman. He was also a ladies' man of the old school and often complimented her on her taste in attire—which was in fact derided by several female columnists as being too demure, too retro, pillbox hat, gloves, more knee-length skirts than pants. But as usual likely voters approved, males overwhelmingly; females by 59.3 percent (though the breakdown by category showed wide variations according to age and/or marital status).

That Phyllis had no history was a problem in a campaign crawling with investigative reporters anxious to find and expose the secret every candidate, every human being, kept closeted, and destroy him/her irrespective of ideology, but they were frustrated this time out, for Ransome's sin was only gluttony (deep-fried snacks); Sloan was wont to claim disgraces he had never committed; and Phyllis had no prior existence.

"We've got to concoct something, Phyl," Pierce told her. "We'll have to come up with a credible past that even our own people will believe genuine, and we can't take anyone else into our confidence."

"You're forgetting Janet," Phyllis pointed out. "And you certainly can get Cliff to support any story you construct. Cliff surely has access to some men who even in this candid era want to be discreet about their private lives."

Pierce had put both these persons on the payroll, Janet as Coordinator of Women's Affairs and Cliff as general consultant. The latter was feeling better since Pierce had introduced him to the gay Sloan ex-aide Jameson Webb. "Okay, Janet, Cliff, and Cliff's friends can provide next-door neighbor accounts of your childhood, but some real places must be named, specific addresses, and what about the other people who were living there at the supposed time? And what of school records?"

"I'll get on that right away."

Phyllis was good as her word. By the following day she had a formulation. "Ellery, I don't have to remind you that unless you reprogram me, I am obliged to tell the truth. But you and all the rest of our team can enjoy the normal human exercise of lying whenever it suits your purpose. I will refuse to speak of my childhood. You, Janet, Cliff, and company can leak my reason for that refusal: I was the victim of a continuing incestuous relationship into which I was coerced at a young age by a family member."

"Who got away with it."

"Who died in prison. Of cancer, painfully."

"And you don't want ever to talk about it, so as not to bring shame to your surviving relatives and to your home town, school, church, et cetera."

"That's about the size of it, Ellery."

"But the media can locate the hometowns of Janet and Cliff and the others."

"There may be some speculation," said Phyllis. "But what

concerns us is only what effect the story will have on probable voters. Most will be sympathetic and will have a negative reaction to any attempt to embarrass me. So I have concluded, combining what I have learned from an observation of human nature and my study of the popular culture of the last half-century."

"I'll also have the matter of our marriage taken care of, registered legally someplace, in case investigative reporters want to verify it. You don't have to be concerned with any of this stuff, Phyl," said Pierce. "I'm not going to change your obligation to tell the truth. It puts the rest of us on our mettle as liars."

"I cannot understand that statement at all," said Phyllis. "But then, I don't have to."

At first, Phyllis's entrance into the race had the effect of boosting Governor Jack Ransome's ratings in the polls. Though an extremely dull candidate of the kind that both major parties helplessly nominated from time to time, Ransome was at least an alternative to Joe Sloan, who, exploiting the rare advantage of having a partisan majority in both houses of Congress, had effectively called for doubling federal expenditures for defense and social programs while cutting taxes in half. The result was unprecedented prosperity in his first two years and an ever-worsening recession that began in the third.

As distractions Sloan threatened several small African and Caribbean nations, who ignored him, and instigated another sex scandal, but the public remained blasé, even when the First Lady pretended to throw down the last straw and leave him for a while, taking their three youngest children to an undisclosed location, thought to be the Adirondacks. All four had only just returned before the White House dinner to which Phyllis and Pierce were invited.

Phyllis's poll numbers did not begin to rise until the supermarket tabloid *The Informer* published their exposé of her. When word of it was first leaked to Pierce, he feared he had waited too long to make his own move, but such fears proved groundless. *The Informer* account, headlined IS PHYLLIS A NYMPHOMANIAC?, did not contain a hint of the real story but rather revealed that she had once danced at a strip club and later worked for a phone-sex business, then supposedly went highbrow with a theatrical production of *Macbeth*, which however was famous for its sex scenes. Of her subsequent movies, only those that emphasized nudity were successful at the box office.

If it had been *The Informer*'s purpose to discredit Phyllis (as apparently it was, for the paper was owned by a born-again type who avidly supported the priggish Ransome), the attempt had the reverse effect. Her numbers thereafter climbed. Males were reminded that she was one hot babe, and many women, their indignation fanned by a Janet-organized group of fierce feminists, professed to have been enraged at such a sexist attack on a woman who, after all, had only earned an honest living from the disgusting weaknesses of men.

Now that Phyllis was proving an ever more dangerous threat, next it was the President's forces that tried to discredit her on the initiative of First Lady Amber Sloan, who through confidential channels instituted a whispering campaign, echoes of which could be heard in a well-known gossip column, to the effect that Phyllis might be overfond of her fellow-woman. But a Howell Fairchild–launched investigation, the results of which were released to certain influential journalists he had cultivated for years, established that the so-called evidence for the charge consisted only of bad-mouthings by Howard Kidd, with whose provincial theater group Phyllis had done *Macbeth* years before and who had since been dumped by his rich wife and indicted for statutory rape of a girl who played Juliet in one of his productions.

The Sloan camp had more success by emphasizing, whenever possible, that Phyllis had devoted her life to her successive careers and, unlike Amber Sloan, who had borne and raised four children, was childless and thus alien to the concept of family that had to a large degree supplanted or anyway vitiated the previous rage for a womanhood of accomplishment beyond nursery or kitchen.

When the polls and focus groups showed a drop in Phyllis's support among young married women, Pierce said, "There's not enough time left for me to make an animatronic child. We got too late a start, Phyl."

"But how about an artificial pregnancy, Ellery?"

"Oh, I guess I could pad your belly, increasing its size regularly, but then what? You would be scheduled to deliver the baby around Election Day. I don't have enough time for both the campaign and fabricating an animatronic child, not to mention that under media scrutiny such an infant would need to be replaced every few weeks with a slightly larger model, with more hair, et cetera—a massive job, Phyl."

"A fake pregnancy could be terminated by a simulated miscarriage, no?"

"Of course—given the stresses of the campaign, what could be more understandable? The outpouring of sympathy would be overwhelming. For several weeks you would be immune to criticism on any issue."

"Moreover," Phyllis pointed out, "the miscarriage would be brought on by the vicious negative attacks of my opponents."

Pierce shook his head in admiration. "Phyllis, you're too much!"

"I thought I was just right," said she. "Else you would make adjustments."

When Pierce asked the advisory committee for the names of possible candidates for vice president, there were no ready suggestions.

This did not surprise Phyllis. "I've researched this subject, Ellery. Running mates are normally lifelong members of a party, notable for their loyalty to it. Though they may have been, up to that point, of the faction that earlier opposed the person now nominated for the big job, they are expected henceforth to join hands in partisan unity against the enemy, uncomplainingly assuming the Presidential candidate's exact position on every issue, especially those that were most fiercely debated during the nominating process by these two very individuals. The reward for the resulting hypocrisy is that the ticket-partner of a victorious President generally has an inside track for his own future bid for the White House."

"Where does that leave our problem, Phyl?"

"We have no party, and thus far I have not expressed an opinion on any issue, so these matters need not be taken into the equation. We can promise a potential vice-presidential candidate that he will have a great opportunity to run on his own eight years from now."

Pierce approved of Phyllis's certainty that she would win the election. With human candidates it is impossible to tell whether their obligatory assurance is sincere or simulated, but as a creation of artifice, Phyllis could afford genuine convictions.

"You're saying we have much to offer. But our panel of experts can't think of anybody to whom the opportunity might appeal. You see, Phyl, the professionals consider the lack of a party a detriment to anyone looking forward to a career in politics."

"Of course," said she. "They are all hacks. What's needed here, Ellery, is thinking outside the box. We don't want a career politician with ambitions of his own. We want a regular person, for whom the idea of running for vice president would be entertaining, something different anyway. Whether he campaigns will be irrelevant to the outcome. In office, I will hardly require his services. Aside from presiding over the Senate, he can play golf or fish or whatever he wants to do."

As outlandish as the idea sounded when first heard, it became more sensible the longer Pierce considered it. When the committee finally came up with suggested candidates, they were either worn-out has-beens of one party or the other; now-obscure former military leaders; or in one case an eccentric ex-president of an Ivy League university, Zoroastrian, bike-riding, clog-wearing.

"Let's face it," said Howell Fairchild, his white eyebrows rising, "the offer simply does not attract anyone of much potential." He smiled benignly. "For the reasons previously stipulated."

Munro T. Wentworth, a pharmacist in a little village in southern Illinois, became Phyllis's running mate when, suffering from one of the headaches that were routine on the campaign trail, Pierce stopped off to buy Nuprin at Wentworth's drugstore.

"Nice little shop you've got here. I haven't ever seen a real soda fountain before." There was even a pair of those elongated glass globes, hanging from chains, in the show window, one filled with orange-colored fluid, the other with green.

"You wouldn't want to make me an offer?" asked the druggist, a comb-over man with a fringe of gray hair and a snub nose. He looked to be in his late forties.

"You're being underpriced out of business by the chain pharmacy at the mall."

"I shouldn't admit that if I want to sell the store," Wentworth sheepishly confessed, "but yes."

"I'll make you a better offer," said Pierce.

Wentworth was not as amazed as he might have been, or again perhaps it was rather that he was simply not demonstrative. Whichever, such a low level of emotional energy was all to the good for the role he was being given. With equanimity he accepted the condition that he would remain almost as unobtrusive as he had been as a pharmacist, his reward being a campaign expense account more generous than the revenue his store had brought in in recent years. He didn't even require his wife's permission. She had wanted to leave town for the past decade.

"And don't worry about the debate, if any," Pierce assured him. "If there is one, you'll be coached beforehand. Meanwhile, we'll furnish you with a standard speech, to be delivered at the places on the itinerary we'll draw up. Your greatest asset is that you've actually done something in real life, unlike either of your opposite numbers, career politicians."

Phyllis had yet to state a policy on any issue, Pierce and the advisors, including foremost among them canny old Howell Fairchild, having determined that an inexperienced candidate did better to say too little than too much. No one has ever had to eat unuttered words, and no matter how late a position is taken, it can usually be defended as preferable to a rash rush to judgment. "Let 'em yap," said Fairchild, "as long as the window of opportunity hasn't closed. The secret's in knowing when to drop the ax."

Pierce had to clarify some of these figures of speech for Phyllis, while urging her never to use them while ad-libbing, lest she inadvertently get into Ransome-like flaps. The governor had on several occasions innocently employed an expression that might have been acceptable in another context than the one at hand, but to say that a black cloud hung over the Sloan economy offended an African-American interviewer, and many persons of short stature found insulting Ransome's insistence that the few foreign-policy accomplishments of Sloan's five-foot Secretary of State were dwarfed by his many shortcomings.

When Phyllis, along with Sloan, was challenged to a series of debates by Governor Ransome, her camp waited for the President's reaction. Sloan was not at full strength in such a situation. He excelled only when he could take an initiative, but was often at a loss with topics chosen by others. In the three debates with General Ralph Wellington, his opponent in the first campaign, the judgment of most media analysts was that Sloan had lost a good two and a half. He had boned up on issues of defense, hoping at least to hold his own against the expert Wellington, but felt betrayed when, during the first debate, military matters were all but neglected in favor of national health policy—and the general scored big with an unexpected display of concern for those both poor and ill while Sloan spoke in a way that could be interpreted as callous.

The President did no better in succeeding weeks on the subjects of the economy, Social Security, veterans' benefits, the lot. He was credited with the half a victory (more properly, half a loss) when in a discussion of agricultural policy he reminisced warmly of his rural youth, cleaning out stables, plowing the back forty, slopping the pigs, among which was a three-legged hog he named Horace. Wellington thereupon reflected aloud that in one of their previous meetings Sloan had claimed a peculiar sense of small-business problems that derived from those of the laundromat his father had tried to operate at the edge of a big-city ghetto.

"That's right," Sloan agreed. "Summers I was sent out to my country uncle's hard-luck little farm." He then displayed the wit that subsequently got him elected, regardless of his so-called deficiencies as identified by the talking heads. "I cain't say I was ever much of a farmer, but I did acquire one skill there that still comes in handy: I can always reckanize manure."

This thrust got a raucous ovation from his attendant claque and was widely quoted from then on throughout the campaign. The celebrated columnist and pundit Dexter Halliday spent Election Day evening in General Wellington's hotel suite, and his report on this experience gained him still another Pulitzer nomination. When the outcome was clear, along about midnight, Wellington shook his mane of snowy hair and addressed his wife, who was of his own age but looked a decade younger. "Mother, we went to an awful lot of trouble only to prove that politics is what I always thought it was: horseshit."

Howell Fairchild believed it likely that Sloan would pass up the debates altogether this time. There was no legal requirement that they be held, and the polls regularly suggested that few watched them and fewer were influenced. Elaine DeMillo, a leading member of Phyllis's team and an early defector from Ransome's when a series of his gay-bashing golf-course jokes were overheard by a caddy and reported, urged Phyllis to participate in the debates only if Sloan did so as well. But Fred O'Casey, veteran of almost as many campaigns as Fairchild, advised her to take the opposite course and debate only if the President did not.

"Those two are always at odds," Pierce noted privately to Phyllis. "Maybe we ought to ease one or the other out."

"That would not be wise," said Phyllis. "Each is very bright. Having opposing points of view on hand provides equilibrium."

"It just makes me uncomfortable that they don't like each other."

"On the contrary, they are in love."

"*What?* Isn't Elaine a Lesbian?"

"Certainly not. She and Fred have been romantically connected since the campaign began and are planning to get married after my victory. Opposites attract, Ellery. Politically she's an idealist, while Fred is a pragmatist."

"How do you know such things, Phyllis?"

"Girl talk."

"I hope *you* don't exchange girlish confidences."

"Hardly," Phyllis said. "I'm running for the Presidency."

"Then she doesn't know you're pregnant. Which reminds me, it's time your belly begins to thicken."

"That's your job, Ellery."

It was the sharp-eyed columnist Inez Goldwyn who first, as a half-joke, asked whether Phyllis, though campaigning vigorously in coast-to-coast whistle-stop swings, had managed to gain weight or had, remarkably at such a time, become pregnant? A few weeks thereafter, it was no longer a question.

Wearing expectant-mother attire, a tails-out blouse under which her abdomen was mounded, Phyllis made the announcement at a news conference attended by clamorous media personnel, who subsequently reacted according to the persuasions of their respective front offices. Running for President while carrying a baby was either a mockery of human values or a celebration thereof; an astonishingly cynical political device or a heartwarming statement of fecundity as opposed to the cold quest for power; the ascendancy of office over family or absolutely vice versa.

Phyllis's ratings rose or fell throughout the constituencies, going higher among Hispanics, African Americans (with whom since early on she had already been the front-runner), and, somewhat surprisingly to most of her team, gay men; whereas she lost some support from Lesbians, a good deal from born-again Christians, and all of the little she had hitherto enjoyed with orthodox Jews, who were basically in Ransome's pocket. The split between the homosexes, though mysterious to Howell Fairchild who dated from a time when such matters were kept discreet, was easily explained by Elaine DeMillo: gay men were notoriously sentimental about motherhood; Lesbians were not.

In sum, however, a pregnant Phyllis, who had regained with a vengeance her former support by the soccer moms, soon had climbed from her flat-bellied 19 percent to 25, taking most points from Governor Ransome, still leading at 38, with the President now at 32. If these figures held, the current 5 percent undecided would not make a difference, but of course such numbers never were stable, as Fairchild and O'Casey could affirm from unhappy experiences with early front-runners who were trounced on Election Day.

Pierce still had no confidants but Phyllis. "I know we had decided you would have a miscarriage not long before the election, but—"

"Excuse me, Ellery. If there was a decision, it was yours," Phyllis said. "I only participated in the discussion."

"Quite right, as usual, Phyl. Here's what I'm getting at now: what a shock it will be, with possible negative consequences, if you lose the child you're supposedly carrying. We're getting such a terrific boost from the pregnancy—the latest Gallup puts you now at only two points below Sloan. Zogby calls you one up and closing on Ransome. Furthermore, the expected mudslinging by your opponents has not yet occurred, and in my opinion—supported by both Elaine and Fred along with most of the rest of our team—it may never happen. A pregnant woman is probably immune from personal attack."

Phyllis wore substantial padding, suggesting a hefty infant to come, symbolic of health, strength, and prosperity. She had adopted an appropriate carriage and stride. As with everything else she did, her performance as an expectant mother was flawless. She was sitting now with her trousered legs apart to accommodate the burden above, a slightly coarse posture, but they were alone in their private quarters in the campaign aircraft— that same private jet they had originally planned to buy for Pierce's vacation, way back when.

"If you are now considering that perhaps I should simulate the delivery of a child, remember that in addition to the aforementioned necessity of producing new artificial infants at regular intervals, there's another problem, Ellery. How then could you ever reveal what I am? The American public might accept an animatronic Presidential candidate, but never would it condone the birth of a robot baby."

20

The details of the miscarriage had to be concealed from Phyllis's own team (except of course Janet and Cliff, who needed no explanation), though it proved an easier cover-up during the frenzy of the late campaign than it might have at a time of fewer distractions. The physical procedure consisted only of the removal of padding. For the sake of the imposture, Phyllis stayed out of sight from all for twenty-four hours. As to the doctor and medical facility, Pierce told another story to each member of the inner circle, begging each never to reveal it. When everybody immediately did so to one another, they did not resent but rather admired the skill of this till now inexperienced politico at disqualifying in advance the inevitable leakage to favored outlets.

No two media references agreed, but the mystery if anything only seemed to increase Phyllis's approval by a public that while always eager for news about celebrities invariably applauded their demand for privacy and indignant denunciation of the paparazzi.

The miscarriage was used by each side in the ongoing abortion debate to make its own case, as absurd as that might seem to its opponent: Leave the termination of pregnancy to God, or, Why would God object to abortions when He performs them Himself? Phyllis never announced her own policy on this issue or indeed any other. Commentators at first needled her for her apparent lack of any program whatever, or even a discernible political philosophy, and when this had no effect, moved into broad derision. What kind of hoax was here being imposed on the American electorate?

At a typical rally, after a preliminary hour of rousing band music, a prancing Rockette line of winsome young women in red, white, and blue miniskirts and straw boaters labeled PHYLLIS, and the distribution of balloons, rubber-reeded Bronx-cheer devices on which to blow at any reference to the other Presidential candidates, and clackers and horns for the riotous celebration of every optimistic truism, Phyllis herself would clatter down by helicopter in whichever landing space was offered, sometimes so constricted as to imperil the crowd.

For such appearances she was attired in action-film costume, metallic bra, gold helmet, molded bronze greaves, short sword at waist, coiled lash in hand. She was body-miked with an impeccable system designed by Pierce himself.

"You all know who I am. [*Horns and clackers, initiated by shills distributed throughout the audience*] I won't waste your time as the others do! [*Flatulent noise of vibrating rubber*] I respect every human being! [*Hitherto unseen placards rise, labeled* PHYLLIS, YOU THE GIRL] I want the best for each American, and I can get it for you. *Everything will be all right.*" With a wave of her gauntleted arm, she would leap back into the helicopter, which quickly rose and made a hummingbird escape toward the horizon.

"Everything will be all right" soon became the popular tag phrase of the moment, widely ridiculed but even more widely repeated, especially by the young, as a kind of involuntary verbal tic. This had been Phyllis's aim, as defined at a strategy meeting with the brain trust, none of whose members, including even Pierce, had at first agreed with her contention that such a platitudinous pseudo-statement could have any but a deleterious effect.

"My study of past Presidential campaigns suggests otherwise," she had said. "People usually elect the candidate who is most reassuring, even in a time when there are no specific crises, for it is the nature of citizens of a democracy, as opposed, say, to benevolent despotism, always to expect trouble and concomitantly fear that those in power won't be able to deal effectively with it. 'Everything will be all right' covers all contingencies, the inevitable recessions, the probable scandals, the precedented wars. That its meaning is unfocused is its strength."

In view of Phyllis's consistent rise in the polls, the others usually deferred to her wishes in the end, and so they did now. If it didn't work it could be dropped without damage, Howell Fairchild pointed out. He was relied on ever to provide the pragmatic compromise that could amicably settle a difference, and throughout a long career he never acquired a serious enemy.

By the end of September, Phyllis had pulled ahead of Sloan and was nipping at Ransome's heels. Four of five nightly panelists on cable were anti-Phyllis, including an acid-tongued right-wing female, a defensive ex-cabinet member of a former liberal administration for which no one nowadays had a good word, and an amiable English emigré with what, always to the delight of his intimidated American colleagues, he called twaddle.

———

After wrangling for many months on the matter, representatives of the three Presidential candidates at last agreed on a series of three debates, two in late October, the final one on the very eve of the election.

Governor Ransome was universally declared by the media to be the clear winner of the first two, giving as he did a structured and measured response to every question. He was moderate on taxes yet not opposed to focused social programs; he called for a powerful military but not one that squandered money on comic-book fantasy weapons; he characterized himself as a "militant peacemonger," but threatened to demolish any rogue nation that challenged his sincerity. His boldest stance was on the issue of abortion: hands off. He was both pro-life and pro-choice, or neither. Let 'em battle it out, the American way.

The foregoing policy or lack thereof was not enunciated until the final debate, the night before the second Tuesday in November. It was clear to the pundits why he had waited so long, but not understandable why he had taken such a position at all, offending both sides on a matter in which there was no middle. One theory held that by the end of the campaign he had cracked under the obligation to please everybody that had throughout his career masked a fundamental disdain for the public, reporters ever having found him cold and rude when the cameras were off.

President Joe Sloan appeared to be drunk at the first debate, but it was universally assumed that as usual he was giving a performance intended to amuse and divert. He swayed violently, clutching the lectern, spouting gibberish, and at one point he belched loudly. At several others, he vigorously scratched his crotch. He lip-farted and blew his nose twice, one nostril at a time, sans handkerchief.

The polls next day were devastating. Not only had no one bought his act, but almost everybody polled had been offended by the implication that he was entertaining.

A transformed Sloan came to the second debate. Now he was tight-buttocked and gimlet-eyed. He out-statisticked Ransome at every turn, quoting Dow, Nasdaq, and S&P figures for every day in the third quarter of the second year of his administration, to make a point concerning fiscal philosophy; naming twenty-two different heirloom apples when, in defense of his agricultural policy, he compared the harvest of New York state with that of the Pacific Northwest; and justifying his opposition to a new bomber because of its possibly unreliable landing gear, the deficiencies of which he explained in great technical detail, sneering at a less than vigilant Pentagon that had been consistently praised by Governor Ransome. But most of those polled next day found this performance boring to the point of suffocation and for that matter as phony as his previous appearance. His numbers now hovered on the brink of one digit.

Two hours before the start of the third debate, the White House physician announced that the President had been put to bed with a respiratory complaint at Walter Reed Memorial. He was not in danger, but he could speak only with difficulty. Vice President Dean Forsythe was offered as a substitute, but the League of Women Voters, debate sponsors, declined.

Therefore Governor Ransome debated, if it could be called that, with only Phyllis. He was more extravagant than he had ever been before, now that an opportunity had been presented to him, in Sloan's absence, to claim the spotlight, but with awkward body language and a nonresonant tenor, he had few gifts as a performer, and though he could pretend to some successes in his own state on education, prescription drugs, and penal reform, they had been diluted by an apparently contradictory rise in both the personal income tax and the deficit, which was pointed out by a waspish, toupeed member of the attendant panel of journalists, to whom Ransome's response was an ad hominem attack on his opposition.

Phyllis was hostilely received by all panelists, as in fact she had been from the first. They made no effort to conceal their disdain for a Presidential candidate who advanced no specific policies on any issue, but their colleagues had gotten nowhere taking this tack on the previous two occasions, Phyllis's ratings having continued to rise, most notably on the morning that followed each debate. So the target now became how her campaign was financed, a matter President Sloan too had questioned previously and into which he threatened to order an inquiry. She claimed to take contributions from only individuals at the grass roots, but could it be true that—as Charles Cookson Bly had suggested in his syndicated column, influential inside the Beltway and among his own colleagues—certain corporations had provided thousands of their employees with sub rosa funds with which to make small personal contributions?

Phyllis was asked different forms of the same question by everyone on the panel, a practice that was permitted by the moderator, the network anchor Chick McCarry, who, responding to criticism next day, said he did so because she never answered it on any occasion.

Of the ever-growing majority of the American people who liked and trusted Phyllis, many in man-on-the-street interviews and focus-group sessions were most impressed by her at least visible immunity not only to outright attack but also to irony, sarcasm, and innuendo on the part of a smart-ass media that they resented. Apparently nothing could throw her off her stride, cause her the least self-doubt, or occasion any excuse or even an explanation.

Yet such assurance was not seen as at all arrogant. Phyllis was a regular guy and genuine, unlike Sloan, who while still a novelty in his first campaign had called himself a "good Joe," and very different from Ransome, whose efforts to relate to the average citizen by visiting discount stores and NASCAR races were as painful to watch as they obviously were for him to do. By doing little to curry popular favor, Phyllis gained it, as by saying little and making no specific promises, she was believed by a public that, contrary to the leading social theorists, had grown less rather than more cynical in the years following the establishment of a worldwide Pax Americana by Sloan's predecessor.

When at the close of the third debate Phyllis and Governor Ransome were each given five minutes for a general summing-up statement on why she/he wished to be President and what he/she would do if elected, Phyllis won the coin toss and chose to let Ransome speak first.

The governor talked for six minutes, despite the frequent sound of the buzzer throughout the sixth. Lack of sleep during the final weeks of the campaign had left its mark in the deep furrows of his gaunt cheeks; the right eyebrow, as if frozen in an arch; and his squinty grin, seemingly of pain. He commiserated with everyone who suffered discomfort or inconvenience of any kind. He denounced betrayers of the dream, "whatever their party," and celebrated those for whom hope is ever fresh. He promised no military adventures but again warned any enemy that retaliation would be swift and devastating. He applauded the uncommon man or woman who each citizen was when the chips were down, when push came to shove, when the pedal meets the metal. He closed with a humble request to be granted the great privilege of serving as "your partner in the task before us." That section of the audience which had come only to cheer him did so on its feet, resoundingly.

Phyllis wore a navy-blue skirt suit, a string of pearls, and only minimal makeup, but her hairdo was somewhat softer, fluffier than usual. Her lectern was a foot lower than that of Ransome, who by contrast seemed loutishly tall.

"I have waited till now to explain the phrase I have repeated throughout the campaign," said she. "'Everything will be all right.' What it means is simply that as President what I do will always make sense. Being more specific at this time would *not* make sense, as making any further promises would not. My study of history has revealed that the one element central to any presidency is chance. Crises inevitably appear as if from nowhere, sneak attacks, invasions, recessions, scandals. Finger-pointing follows for partisan motives, but the worst calamities could probably not have been foreseen. All that matters is what's done about them. In my case I have no party to serve, no debts to pay, no favors to return. My only cause is to make sense.

"Now, I am aware that in each recent presidential election fewer people have voted than did the time before. That so many do not vote has been universally deplored, though not casting a vote is only to exercise one of the sacred rights of a citizen of a democracy, as important as any other. So here I am, urging each of you to do as you wish tomorrow, to vote or not. If you have something more satisfying to do, drinking yourself into a stupor, having promiscuous sex, playing games of chance, et cetera, do it with my blessing. If you vote, it would make sense to vote for me."

———

Phyllis was the first write-in candidate to be chosen by American voters as Chief Executive, as well as the first woman. She was also the first animatronic President-elect, though that fact was still unknown to every human being but Pierce, Janet, and Cliff. Her strength in the South astonished the Northeast, and vice versa, both regions regarding themselves as uniquely stalwart defenders of underdogs, whereas among Californians the assumption was always that everyone else followed their lead, and in this case they were right, Phyllis losing only Hawaii and Alaska, the inhabitants of which were still defensive about being as full-fledged Americans as the citizens of the contiguous forty-eight and tended to cast their votes for the orthodox parties.

There were as many regulations concerning write-in votes as there were states of the Union, and even before the returns were officially tallied, fifty legal challenges were filed by the losers. Was a ballot legitimate if "Philis" was written on it, or "Filos" or "Phylas"? And what of "Phallus" and "Feelass"? Should the obvious satire of "Fool Us" be counted? The highest courts of every state were busy with these matters, while the U.S. Supreme Court waited on call and the media commentators, not fazed in the least by their universal failure to predict Phyllis's victory, filled their columns and/or airtime with confident second-guessing that often concerned what the newly named first Asian-American justice would do. When one talking blonde called Kenneth Wong "inscrutable," she was assailed as a bigot and required by her network to apologize for racial insensitivity.

As it turned out, only the state decision on the contested returns in Idaho, favorable to Phyllis, reached the Supreme Court, and Wong voted with the six-three majority to accept it. After such a precedent, the other challenges were dropped and Phyllis was in every sense of the word the authentic President-elect of the United States of America.

21

The weeks between the election and Inauguration Day were emotionally an elongated morning-after for Pierce.

"I still can't really believe it."

"You've said that again and again, Ellery. Is it your purpose to be forever astonished or do you think you'll eventually come to believe in whatever it is you question?"

"Your election, Phyllis: I can't believe it happened, though it was my idea. What was not my idea was that on which you ran. Nor was it that of our skilled campaign advisors. It was yours. I made you, but you've gone far beyond what I thought was your capacity. I don't understand anything any more."

"Aren't you forgetting a basic truth of everything human, which properly includes all that is made by human beings, that a whole is greater than the mere sum of its parts?"

"Frankly, whenever I accept the situation, I get cold feet. I get scared, Phyl. You are talented, but how in the world can you handle the Presidency? You've got no party and therefore no real influence in Congress. You'll be commander-in-chief of the armed forces, but what plans do you have for the military? You said nothing about minority matters during the campaign, yet most minorities voted for you despite the pandering to them of Sloan and Ransome." He groaned. "And speaking of Sloan, there are rumors that he might refuse to leave office. I think Joe himself may have started the rumor as one final hoax, but still it's disturbing. After all, till January twentieth *he* commands the armed forces."

"No problem," said Phyllis. "FBI Director Santos has check-ed that out. So we won't have to kill President Sloan."

"Very funny," said Pierce. "Wait a minute—you've spoken to Santos?"

"He came to see me yesterday, Ellery. I assumed you knew that. He wants to keep his job under my administration."

Until they moved into the White House, they were staying at the estate Pierce had leased in northern Virginia. Scores of staffers were ever present, as were the Secret Service agents who guarded Phyllis. Since Pierce would make sure she never left the property until the Inauguration, it would be easy to keep an eye on her. Or so he had believed.

"But I did *not* know, Phyl. When was that, yesterday morning? I was on the phone for hours."

"I didn't see Santos for long. Not being human, I don't waste time. I got the information that enabled me to dismiss the concern about Sloan's rumored coup, and I assured Santos his job was safe."

"You did?"

"There's no justification for incredulity, Ellery. I'm President-elect. To be sure, I cannot lie, but I can mislead."

"What does that mean?"

It might have been his imagination, but since the election

Phyllis seemed to be undergoing a subtle change, which thus far could be called one of tone. She had never suffered from doubt, but she had been essentially self-contained. Now she was increasingly aware of her potential power over others, which after all was guaranteed by the Constitution.

"My meaning is that I spoke literally to Santos. His job *is* safe, for the next two months. When I get into office I shall appoint Rico Santangelo as director of the FBI."

"Phyllis." Pierce spoke gently, to reassure himself. "Surely you aren't referring to the infamous Mafioso, head of the Spadini crime family? I assume you mean a respectable man of the same name. But is it advisable to encourage such a confusion?"

"Don't be foolish, Ellery," Phyllis said with a new edge to her voice. "Who would be more expert on the matter of crime than a ruthless mobster? As who would be more authoritative on the subject of homeland security than Abu Hassan, whom I intend to release from federal prison and appoint to the cabinet post."

Pierce desperately told himself that he had been wrong: Phyllis had somehow developed a sense of humor. Abu Hassan's capture, nine years earlier, had effectively brought to a halt the principal terrorist threat to the USA.

"Phyllis, let me give you a piece of advice. I haven't forgotten that you are President-elect and I'm not. But I created you, and I love you dearly." He could never have imagined that the time would come when he had to massage an animatronic ego. "But while it's okay to joke privately with me about these things, it wouldn't be a good idea to do so with anybody else. There are going to be leaks, no matter how carefully we try to guard against them, and if remarks like these get to your enemies in the media—well, think what Carleton Small or Gwen O'Halloran would make of them."

"Ellery, once again I must remind you that I will soon be commander-in-chief of the greatest military force in the world, also boss of the FBI, ATF, CIA, DEA, IRS, and the Secret Service, to name only part of the power at my beck and call, and I have little tolerance of critics, whom I can simply have killed if they step over the line."

Pierce knew the onset of panic, but he suppressed it by pretending to play along. "Why, sure you could, Phyllis. With a snap of your fingers. Off with his head!"

"I won't have to take any shit from anybody," Phyllis said. "I'll be in charge."

Pierce opted for distraction. "What we have to do now, Phyl, is study the recommendations for appointments and begin to name people to the top posts. It should be easy for you to run through the resumés and pick those with the best qualifications. You won't be obliged to please a political party or any special interests. You'll be the first officeholder not in someone's pocket."

Phyllis displayed an expression of dubiety that he had never programmed. "I think it would make sense to organize a Phyllis Party, Ellery. For the sake of social stability, such power bases are necessary if structures are to be built and maintained. Also, now that I got into power without them, I want to reach out to the special interests, which represent everybody when taken in sum and do not remain special. Mutual backscratching is perfectly reasonable. What we must take care to do is to get back at least a favor and a half for every one we grant. That's how successful governance works."

"Yes, Phyl."

"Let's set up committees to deal with each of the principal minorities, with a catchall to represent the smaller ones,

Lithuanians, Peruvians, et alia, not leaving anyone out of the big tent. And we'll want to connect up with the trial lawyers, the defense contractors, the teachers' union, and big oil—anybody out for a buck or with an ax to grind. I want to be everybody's President. I'm going to bring us all together, the flag-wavers with the flag-burners. We're all Americans."

"Uh, Phyl," said Pierce, "you're American-*made*. With all respect, you're animatronic."

"But you *have* no respect, Ellery. I don't want you to call me Phyl any more, or even Phyllis. I am to be addressed as Madame President."

"I'm aware that you have been left out of much of the picture till now," Pierce said to Munro Wentworth, Vice President–elect. "But that neglect is historical. Franklin D. Roosevelt, though mortally ill, died without telling V.P. Harry Truman anything about the atom bomb."

Wentworth was studying the menu. Pierce had invited him to breakfast in the coffee shop of the hotel in which Wentworth was staying until he and his wife could move into the Naval Observatory after the Inauguration.

"I think I'll go with the Spanish omelet and home fries."

"But the President sees a big role for you once in office."

"On the other hand," Wentworth said, "I wonder if the expense account could handle the breakfast steak? The missus and I have been holding back, you know, but now that our team has won—"

"Munro—if I may call you that, Mr. Vice President–elect— how much executive experience have you had? I know you ran the drugstore, but how about the PTA or the local schoolboard?

Did you ever hold a municipal office? How about some organization like the Kiwanis?"

"Not me," said Wentworth. "I've spent all my time just trying to scratch out a living. Uh, listen, Mr. Pierce, suppose the budget could handle both the steak and a short stack? I haven't had time for a decent feed since the campaign began. At those dinners I'd get two bites of the chicken before I had to give the speech, after which they'd fly me off to the next rally."

"Order the whole damn menu, Munro. Yes, we won and finances are no longer a pressing concern. I mean, for the campaign. The nation's budget is another matter. Did you personally keep the drugstore's books?"

"That was one of my problems," said Wentworth, running an index finger across his clean upper lip, where a mustache could be fitted. Pierce was trying to visualize alterations that might give the man a more authoritative air. But no mustached Presidents had held office for a century past, while hirsute-lipped tyrants, Hitler, Stalin, Saddam Hussein, had abounded. "My brother-in-law did the books. Now, I love my wife, but Nelson Hunnicut was another thing."

A hurried waitress refilled their cups, slopping coffee in Wentworth's saucer. That neither she nor any of the other customers in the coffee shop recognized the man now only a heartbeat away from being future leader of the free world was to be expected. If precedent were followed and he remained Number Two for the next eight years, Wentworth would be no more identifiable to the public than he was now.

"Do you read much, Munro? I mean current events, history?"

The former pharmacist dropped three cubes of sugar into the new cupful, already turned beige by milk. "I was fool enough to think I might find some time for reading once I got out of the store, but I had even less time on this campaign. I didn't even get any sleep." He grimaced. "I might of made the wrong decision, Mr. Pierce. I doubt I'm cut out for politics."

"By the way, Munro, where is the Secret Service?"

"Pardon me?"

"You're supposed to be protected by Secret Service agents."

"That's a new one on me," said Wentworth. "Why?"

"I'll check on that as soon as we get finished here," Pierce told him. Evidently that crack agency had either forgotten Wentworth's existence or at some point mislaid him. "Because, Munro, you might be put on your mettle sooner than you think. That you are ill prepared need not be catastrophic. Once again I'll allude to Harry Truman, who admittedly had a bit more experience in public life, but like you he owned a little Middle American retail business that failed, and he seemed to be a modest man with few of the dramatic qualities of his predecessor. When he suddenly became President, he said it was as if the sky had fallen on him."

The waitress slapped down a plateful of warm toast, and Wentworth peeled back the covering napkin, seized a slice, and wolfed down three-quarters of the triangle in one bite. "Haha!" he managed to crow while still swallowing. "Butter, not margarine." After a drink of coffee he stared at his companion, eyes showing a new spark. "Why do you bring the subject up at this point, Pierce?"

Pierce raised his hands in contrition. "I admit we should have done so long since. I can only plead the unbearable pressures of the campaign. We're going to try to make it up to you from here on."

"It would be nice if I could meet the President-elect just once," Wentworth said. "Get her autograph for my daughter, who's in college now, but was a big fan of those movies as a kid."

"Why, of course. You and Mrs. Wentworth must come to dinner. Phyllis is looking forward to that, as am I."

Wentworth maintained his stare. "I think you've got something more in mind."

"Nothing ulterior, I assure you. If we didn't believe you could do a good job, I would never have picked you."

"Let me tell you about myself," Wentworth said. "We never had much crime in our little town, but a stranger came in the store a few years back, asked me to change a dollar for the phone outside, but when I opened the register he says, 'While you're there, take out all the money and hand it over.' I looked up and saw he had a pistol on me. Now, I kept a gun of my own on the shelf just below the register, never had to touch it in all those years, but I ducked down, grabbed it, and came up firing. He took two quick shots at me at that close range but missed. I got off two rounds of my own. One took off the tip of an ear, and the other went right through his eye."

"Jesus," said Pierce. "We should have known about that. Wonder the tabloids missed it. Hard to say where the advantage would have gone: to the gun lobby or to those who want to disarm everybody but criminals. Anyway, thanks for telling me now."

Wentworth turned out to be a tough little bastard. He would do.

"Ellery, where have you been? I don't want you to go anywhere without first getting my permission."

"I thought I told you, Ph—Madame President-elect." They were in her high-ceilinged office at the Virginia mansion, to gain entrance to which from the Secret Service agents, who knew him well, he now had to be rigorously searched and furnish multiple IDs. "I thought it only right to welcome the Vice President–elect into the fold. He's been totally neglected."

"Fuck that loser," said Phyllis. "Nothing's going to happen to me, and as to his presiding over the Senate, I intend to cut that bunch out of the loop as much as I can. What do they accomplish for the good of the nation? Building pork-barrel post offices for rednecks who can't read and billion-dollar highways connecting Nowheresvilles to a chain of swamps?" Phyllis had pulled her hair back into a tight bun, and she wore no makeup. She was attired in an all-black, ankle-to-throat jumper, a kind of ninja uniform that perhaps derived from one of her films, though if so, it was the costume of a heavy.

"Uh," said Pierce, "there's the little matter of the Constitution."

"I'm going to pack the Supreme Court," Phyllis said. "Then there'll be no problem."

"Are that many justices about to retire?"

She smiled. "Ellery, little by little I've come to realize you have a second-rate sensibility. Oh, you know your way around technology, but that's about your limit. I can see why you never succeeded with human women. Inferior as they are, they could still easily get your number."

He shrugged. "That's true enough."

"You admit it? You see how weak you are? I'm afraid you're a born bootlicker, Ellery. You're not much of a man, even by low human standards."

Pierce was stung. "Who *is* your idea of a man?"

"President Sloan."

"*Joe Sloan?* That horse's ass?"

"Be careful, Ellery. He's still in office. And I don't like to hear a President disrespected."

"I thought you despised him too."

Phyllis pursed her lips. "I've come to realize what the Presidency calls for. We're a special breed, we whom the American people have selected to lead them. The differences amongst us are trivial compared to what we all, from George Washington on, share." She raised the chin he had sculptured. "No layman could ever understand." She cleared her throat for rhetorical purposes; she was immune to catarrh. "I shall name ex-President Sloan as the new Chief Justice."

"Well, you're the boss," Pierce said. "May I respectfully ask what your plans are for me?"

"Ellery," Phyllis said, "if you remember, I did very well when entirely on my own. In fact I became an international movie star. You played no part whatever in that accomplishment. During the same period you became a derelict and lived underneath a freeway bridge. You wouldn't be here today, so close to the center of world power, had I not saved your bacon."

"True enough."

"The situation now is such that you have become more of a hindrance than a help. I don't want to hear your puny objections to every measure I take as Supreme Commander, and as to your practical value, after years of observing your techniques, I am quite capable of maintaining myself interminably. Ironically enough—and by the way I have finally developed a sense of irony; being elected President did the trick—you built me to be indestructible." She showed the radiant smile for which he had equipped her with teeth molded from a polymer superior in every quality to God's product, as bright as when they were installed and never since stained by red wine, tobacco, or time.

"Yes, ma'am."

"I need a consort better suited to my new station," said Phyllis. "There is one way you can be useful, Ellery, and in so doing perpetuate your own life." She smiled as brightly as ever while making this sinister threat, still another reminder, if he still required one, that she was not weakened by a conscience. "The Secret Service has kept the defunct Tyler Hallstrom. I want you to overhaul and reactivate him."

Though he had already determined what to do, Pierce could not resist asking, "How are you going to justify taking a First Husband that the public already knows is animatronic?"

"I don't have to justify anything I do to anybody," said Phyllis. "Now, no more questions if you know what's good for you."

"Phyllis," Pierce said, "please let me address you by that name for the last time. It's very dear to me. I know you despise sentimentality, but I suspect that when all is said and done it's the fundamental human trait of everyone mortal, be they saints or villains, probably installed by *our* Maker—for your benefit, a divine Ellery—in whom I more or less believe though my under-god is technology."

She scowled. "You're running off at the mouth, Ellery. You've been doing that for years, but I won't tolerate any more of it."

"I first really fell in love with you only after you left me, when you were no longer under my control, though I had built you to be submissive."

"You have only yourself to blame now. It was your idea I go into politics."

"I take full responsibility. I have no regrets. And let me say I have never loved and admired you more than I do at this moment."

"That's your limitation. If you had any spine you would fight back, even though you couldn't possibly win. 'The time of life is short; / To spend that shortness basely were too long.' William Shakespeare's *Henry the Fourth, Part One*, Act Five, Scene Two."

"Easy for you to say, Phyllis."

"You've called me that twice now, Ellery. Obviously, you are incorrigible and must be dealt with harshly."

"I've gone as far as I'm going," Pierce said. "I will not resuscitate Hallstrom. I understand what the consequences will be, and I'm ready to accept them." He smiled tenderly at her. "It's been quite a ride, Phyllis. If given the opportunity I would do it all over again. Just let me kiss you good-bye, for old times' sake."

She shook her sneering head. "As you well know, I only do things that make sense."

All this while he had been standing before her desk, as if on trial. "It won't compromise your power. It's just a civilized way in which to part, and let me tell you this, Phyl, you can't disregard all civility. That would be unprofessional and inspire a certain contempt."

She made an extra blink apart from the regular ones for which she had been programmed. Perhaps only he who had made her could have seen it. He had not quite lost all his claim on her. But still she resisted.

"You think you know everything, Ellery. It's very tiresome."

"Just one farewell kiss, Phyl. Then I'll be out of your hair for good."

She impatiently waved him off, while nevertheless saying, "Oh, all right. Make it quick."

He went around the desk. That she did not accommodate him by turning in the chair so that he could put his lips on hers was all to the good for his real purpose.

He bent and lightly kissed her left cheek, at the same time inserting the tip of his little finger into her nearby ear and pressing the tiny fail-safe button just inside the auditory orifice, an essential of the original design but never used till now. Had it not functioned after all those years he might have been a goner. But in fact it worked perfectly.

Phyllis froze in position, her disdainful expression in place, hands folded in her lap. The natural-looking light in her eyes had been replaced by a small red LED in each, like that of a power-on answering machine or stereo.

Pierce spoke as if she were sentient, though he could not be sure she was, never having tested the device and not daring to switch it off now to check.

"Forgive me, Phyllis. You gave me no choice. Allowing you to lead this country in your current state would be ruinous, and it would ultimately have been all my own doing. I would have become the mad scientist of the old horror movies instead of what I am, a romantic with stars in his eyes. . . . My work is cut out for me now. I'll have to forge a doctor's death certificate and arrange a state funeral. I think Wentworth, after his initial shock, might very well rise to the challenge and make a decent President."

He stepped away from her. She was not dead, but being near her in her current limbo made him uneasy, considering all they had been to each other . . . and might be again, if he could work the bugs out of what was manifestly a winning design.

Adventures of the Artificial Woman is THOMAS BERGER's twenty-third novel. His previous novels include *Best Friends*, *Regiment of Women*, *Neighbors*, and *The Feud*, which was nominated for a Pulitzer Prize. His *Little Big Man* is known throughout the world.